TORMENTED
VIRGIN

TORMENTED
VIRGIN

JOHN D. KEEFAUVER

with an introduction by
BRIT MANDELO

and an editor's afterword by
SCOTT NICOLAY

LETHE PRESS

First edition published in 1962 by Epic Books/Art Enterprises, Inc.
This new edition published in 2019 by Lethe Press, Inc.
www.lethepressbooks.com • lethepress@aol.com
isbn: 978-1-59021-627-9 / 1-59021-627-X

Set in Garvis, Century Gothic, and Century Old Style.
Interior design: Alex Jeffers
Cover art: James O'Barr
Cover design: Inkspiral Design

Library of Congress Cataloging-in-Publication Data available on request.

CONTENTS

INTRODUCTION • Brit Mandelo   ix

TORMENTED VIRGIN   1

WHAT MAD PURSUIT? • Scott Nicolay   139

INTRODUCTION

BRIT MANDELO

Texts provide, often, an angle: an approach to a moment in time, a reflection of a gestalt. That sticks for pulp smut as much—if not more than—highbrow art; in the popular imagination, in the presumed privacy of the sexy dime novel, what do writers and readers think of gender, sexuality, and intimacy? John D. Keefauver's *Tormented Virgin* is one of a thousand of these "specials," originally published in 1962 as an Epic Original (#126). The novel follows Gene through his romance with the young and attractive Faye, as well as his attraction to Mickey—the lesbian who is attempting to bring Faye over to the dark side, as it were—and Mark, his own best friend. This confusion of gender and attraction creates a subversively queer milieu for a novel that, in the end, attempts to glorify the "solution" of Gene and Faye coupling up and conquering their bisexual urges to be straight together.

The result, then, is that *Tormented Virgin* presents a fascinating take on the cultural mores of the early sixties in terms of bisexuality, though it certainly doesn't intend to do so. A bit like the mosquito in amber, this text offers a direct representation of a male writer's take, for a presumed male audience, on bisexual attraction and its dangers. It is, as one might expect, full of strange and raw ideas about the conflation of gender with sexuality and a whole set of (frankly misogynist) approaches to women's attractions. It certainly doesn't intend to present a queer foursome as a potential positive relationship. However, considering that the vast majority of the text explores bisexual attraction for taboo sensuality and tension—until the very last few pages, when straight sex wins through!—*Tormented Virgin* ends up undermining its own argument at most turns. It's a bit of a stretch, after all, to convince the reader that there's something wrong with Faye and Mickey or Gene and Mark when the reader has been getting off to the tension between the queer pairs and the "will they or won't they?" of it for the whole book. This in and of itself is perhaps the most intriguing accidental revelation of Keefauver's novel: the sexual energy of the text is struggling against queerness but subsumed to it, constantly, and the twist at the end doesn't ring particularly true as a result.

On one level, for a contemporary queer reader, this is just another offensive representation of bisexuality as confusion, of lesbians as predatory half-men, and of queer men as diffident, feminine, and ineffective. To conquer queerness for Gene is to become masculine; to refuse queerness for Faye is to become feminine; these are presented as the clear and obvious successes of the text, with the assistance of therapy to become "normal" for Faye. It's a whole mess of unpleasant tropes packed tight together. Sexuality is conflated with gender in direct and nonnegotiable terms; as the novel goes, the part of Faye that is attracted to Mickey is the part of her that is a man, and the part of Gene that is attracted to Mark is the part of him that is a woman. Both are presented in the text as occupying an in-between gender due to their bisexuality.

However—and this is the significant *however*—this is also a text published in 1962 for popular readers, a pulp audience. As such, it's a direct articulation of the cultural norms surrounding queer sexuality in the mainstream. The angles it provides to a contemporary critic, then, are twofold: the first, as a text that queer readers have the opportunity to coopt for its destabilization of gender and sexuality in its search for erotic tension; the second, as a commentary on the evolving perceptions of gender and attraction in the public conscious in the early sixties. The third angle, of course, is the one that would have us discard the book entirely; that it's pulp trash with an offensive viewpoint that doesn't jive with current articulations of identity—but the one doesn't give us much to work with, and also doesn't give room to examine the nuance of our past via text. It is, ultimately, an unintentionally provocative text; as queer readers, we flatly disagree with its closing arguments but might still find something illuminating and compelling in the conflicts and confluences it reveals without meaning to, in the decentered and strange magneticism queerness seems to have for both of our protagonists.

I, for one, have a hard time believing that one night of traditional heterosexual intercourse between Gene and Faye is going to make them straight—goodbye sexual tension with Mark and Mickey, goodbye the encounter between Faye and the erotic dancer who in contemporary parlance would be considered a genderfuck performer, goodbye all of those scenes in which Gene prefers a woman who isn't "all woman" to dominate him. The text doesn't convince us, certainly, as readers—and that's where the leverage point is for a critic to pluck at the threads of psychological and cultural strain revealed in Keefauver's otherwise eyebrow-raising presentation of a man seducing a woman out of her queerness.

Gene himself, as our protagonist and point of view character, is a fascinating specter of threatened masculinity, confused desire, and homosocial/homosexual longing. As Faye says after they've fooled around in his car, after she's already made a pointed comment about how Gene wants her to be dominant and another about his interest in Mark:

> "You make me feel all woman"
> He chuckled. "You make me feel all man."
> "I told you I'd find out the real reason you
> want to keep seeing me." (37)

He doesn't seem to have a firm grasp—or he refuses to—on the fact that he's attracted to Mark as more than a friend for quite some time in the text, or that the reason both Faye and Mickey give for being attracted to Gene in the first place is that he's, as Mickey later says, "half man, half woman...you got enough woman in you to excite me" (54). This treatment of gender is, from a critical standpoint, both outré and fascinating. Queerness is here given a specific and almost diabolical sort of power: the power to transcend and twist gender, attraction, and relationships. While the text intends this to be alarming and titillating—with, of course, the assumption that it will not be allowed to triumph—for a queer readership there is a subversive thrill as well.

There is also something to be said for the fact that the text does not present us with solely Faye's bisexuality. It shifts the structure of the narrative to include Gene's own struggle with his unacknowledged bisexuality; this is, rather obviously, not the tale of a straight man winning over a queer woman with the lure of his penis. As Faye frequently suggests, to Gene's distinct discomfort, it is a tale of a queer man trying to be straight with a queer woman. The novel itself presents this as desirable, and the conflict is the conflict of resisting erotic relationships with the same gender, but once again: it's a bit difficult to avoid the fact that the conflict *is* the tension *is* the erotic content, and queer desire is therefore central, powerful and dramatic. This is clear in the strip-club scene, where Gene takes Faye to see a performer who does an act in drag: half man, half woman. Both Gene and Faye are aroused at the show; Faye panics, of course, but later returns to the performer to work out some of her attraction to someone like herself, someone she perceives to be "half and half." Gene, too, comes around to admit to himself when Faye pressed him that he isn't actually "sure" he's all man, that he is attracted to masculine women and to men.

There is something distinctly appealing about the genderqueer dualities of these characters, though it is intended as an insult and is the result of a historically accurate but contemporarily problematic treatment of sexuality. At the same time, intention aside, the fact remains that this text presents the reader with two protagonists who consider themselves fundamentally in the middle of a binary gender spectrum. Each articulates being half-man, half-woman; while this is cause for deep concern for them, it's also the source of a significant amount of identification, attraction, and understanding. This exploration of gender—given over as it is to Gene as much as Faye—was the one thing that stuck out the most in this text. It seems, in some senses, that the titular tormented virgin might as well be Gene too: Gene, who hasn't had sex with a man, who is just now articulating his attraction to masculinity. While queer attraction here is presented as a longing for masculinity by a man who isn't man enough, and vice versa, it's still *present*. Imagine the popular context in 1962, and imagine snagging this text from a rack of lurid paperbacks for the girls on the cover then encountering a tale about a man trying to come to terms with and avoid his queerness.

Quite a different thing than the reader might have been looking for—though he might have been soothed by the triumph of heterosexuality in the end, he still spent the whole damn book being pulled back and forth between Gene's attraction to Mark, the masculine Mickey, and the dominant less-feminine side of Faye. The sex scenes in the text are all interestingly queer as well, or nontraditional for their context: Faye's encounters with Mickey, with the genderfuck performer; Gene's being fucked by Mickey, and his erotic encounters with Faye that do not culminate in intercourse. In fact, the single traditional heterosexual encounter in the book is the finale, which both characters have to struggle to achieve and seems, frankly, less pleasurable and erotic than the rest of the sex in the book and more to serve a narrative and psychological purpose—verifying to each that they've come around to straightness.

Again, this isn't particularly convincing.

In a queerer novel, the outcome of this all would perhaps be that Gene, Faye, Mickey, and Mark all get together and have a fine time. Instead, Keefauver must recenter heterosexuality after spending the majority of the text teasing at bisexuality and the lure of same-gender attraction. As a whole, this text isn't particularly special; no critical argument could be made that it stands out from its contemporaries. Rather, the value of examining it and reprinting it comes from the arguments it makes by accident about the cultural and sexual attitude of the early sixties—and for the unintentional and fascinating presentation of a boundary-blurring, gender-scrambling numinous queerness that the characters must struggle against. It's so powerful it cannot be resisted for long. Readers can also examine the snapshot of attitudes to gender and sexuality that strike a contemporary audience as bizarre, outdated, ignorant or cruel. As an example of a specific moment in time—just one of a thousand pulp erotic novels—this one offers us a specific look at gender and sexuality as written for a straight audience... that is perhaps far more queer than intended. To a queer reader at the time, seeking representation or erotic tension, this text might have provided more than it ever thought to. For all these reasons, it's a quick and potentially productive read for contemporary audiences.

TORMENTED
VIRGIN

CHAPTER ONE

It wasn't until he was in bed with Faye Sherritt that Gene Bond panicked. It wasn't until her arms coiled wanting and warm around him that he pushed himself away and sat up on the edge of the bed, his back cold to her glowing young body snuggled under the sheet. He had tried. He had got in bed with her and tried. But since she had told him about herself and her problem he had not, he realized now, wanted to make love to her. More than not wanted; he couldn't.

When they had started for his apartment an hour or so ago he had felt uneasy, an anxiety he had hidden from Faye. He knew that to tell her he didn't want to make love to her would be the worst thing he could do under the circumstances. So he had taken her to his apartment hoping that, when they were in bed and she was soft and close in his arms, his qualms would go. Besides, she had insisted in a desperate plea of anguish.

"Gene," she had said. "Please. Tonight, Gene. I want to. I have to. Please help me, Gene."

They had been sitting in the dark in his car in front of the house where they had just been to a party, and she moved close to him as she pleaded and kissed him in a tender-wanting violence that had finally made him say yes and take her to the apartment.

She was not just a beauty, Faye Sherritt. She was much more. She was a beauty with fire and intelligence and sex, but she would have been a beauty with any one of these alone, and she stayed a beauty when, sometimes, she didn't want to be. Even when she moodily turned off her fire and sex and intelligence, her beauty remained. Perhaps because it was an intelligent beauty that whispered instead of shouted from her lifting, winking breasts, beauty that only murmured from curved hips and thighs, and beauty that carefully said yes from eyes that spoke only when they wanted. And when they wanted, Gene Bond had found out, they got. She had a fire that had flashed for more than twenty years, a flame that had effortlessly gathered moths, all frantic to be burned. Until. Until a few years ago when the fire had sputtered and turned cold and had nearly gone out. Then hesitant, gangling, tuft-haired Gene Bond had come along.

Now, sitting on the edge of the bed, his head dangling toward his bare knees, Gene was mumbling. "I'm sorry, Faye, but I can't. I can't, that's all, I can't."

They had driven directly from the party to his apartment and gone quickly into the bedroom, Faye leading the way. Gene behind, trying to think of some way to postpone the hurt he would give his already injured Faye.

But she had taken off her clothes and stood naked to him in the dark room, waiting for him to come to her. And when he had stood apart, hesitating, she had come to him and took him in with her, in her arms, pressing herself tight against him, murmuring,

"I know what's holding you back, Gene. But I can help you, like you can help me."

No, what she was thinking was not correct, Gene knew. There was something else that was holding him from her. And he couldn't tell her what it was because it would squash all the progress she had made in the last few months.

Murmuring, "Gene, I'm going to try so hard, but you have to help me."

"Yes," he had said.

"Try, Gene."

Then they had lain down beside each other and he had heard her say, "Don't hurt me, Gene. If you hurt me it will be bad. For me," and her arms were around his neck, her lips nuzzled in against his cheek. She had started talking then, tightening her arms, pulling herself in close, her words coming into his ear and his mind, afraid, yet excited and pleading.

"Gene, honey, oh Gene. You're so good to me. So patient. I'm going to try so hard. Let me kiss you. Gene. Kiss me some more. Do that again. I like that. Isn't this right? Like this?'

"Yes."

"Gene?"

"Yes."

"Don't stop, Gene. Why are you stopping?"

"Faye, honey, I..."

"Gene, what are you getting up for? Where are you going?"

"Gene! what's the matter?" he had heard her whisper, her voice like the sound of a moan.

The matter, he thought when his feet were on the floor, was the months of knowing Faye Sherritt. The matter of carrying the weight of her dilemma, and, yes, the matter of the joy, too, he had had in being able to carry her problems, or at least try to. The matter of being attracted to Faye Sherritt, yet at the same time being wary and sometimes even afraid of her. The matter was the memory, the memory that had caught up with him and become now.

His mind began skipping back, back, back over the joys and the problems they had had together. These were the things that mattered. Back into the memory, avoiding—shutting out—these things that did not involve him and Faye—these things that did not matter.

"Gene, tell me what's the matter?" she moaned again, lifting up in almost a jerk onto one elbow.

The matter, he thought, is you.

But after only a moment's hesitation, he added, and me.

CHAPTER TWO

Back to the day they met his memory took him, back to his first week at work earlier in the summer as a reporter on the *Press*. Gene had come from Virginia to take the job in Chelsor on the coast of Lake Michigan. Mark Kierson had introduced him to Faye and Mickey Jessup. Mark, a heavy-set wire editor with hair thinning at the temples, was in his early thirties and a few years older than tall, lanky Gene.

Mickey was the *Press*'s church editor who described a church as a place where it was awfully hard to buy martinis. She talked to the clergy over the phone as if they were bartenders who needed encouragement. She laughed at the churchmen with her throaty, low voice, almost masculine, just as she laughed at Gene's asking for a date that first week he knew her. She told him she was "only interested in men who jump out of airplanes without parachutes. And I doubt," she said, "if you'd jump *with* one."

Aside from knowing that Mickey Jessup's past consisted mainly of husbands, which she informed him of with a *my-God-it-was-hell* expression, Gene knew nothing about her. She was a wiry, lanky woman in her middle twenties, attractive in a sarcastic sort of way, who had lived, with the various husbands, in Chelsor all of her life, so Mark had told him. Gene,

who did general news assignments and at times even
helped Mickey do her church news and women's fea-
tures, had told her from the beginning, jokingly yet
seriously enough, that he would be glad to help her at
night in her apartment, where she lived alone. "Doll,"
she had gurgled, sarcastically. "But no thanks. I don't
do any work in my apartment. Of any kind." And
Gene had felt, for some reason he couldn't pin down
then, relieved.

Mickey had invited him to her apartment after
work one evening for a martini, though. They had
both worked late, and it was getting dark when they
reached her studio-type place. An extremely hot evening, she had opened all the windows and turned on
the fan. Then, turning out the lights and moving to
a sofa next to a window, she casually took off her
blouse and bra and drank her first martini.

"It's not fair," she said. "Men can take off their shirts
when it's hot, why can't women?"

Gene, sitting across from her in the room, could
see the medium rise of her breasts silhouetted against
the window. He finished his drink quickly and moved
over to sit beside her on the sofa. She didn't object
when he began to caress her breasts, but she didn't respond either. She kept on drinking her martini as he
bent and kissed the soft rounded flesh, tanned from
lying naked on the beach and swimming in Lake
Michigan.

"You're wasting your time, buster," she said as his
tongue flicked over her. "I swore off men a long time
ago."

He tried to push her down on the sofa, but she
whacked him where it hurts, and he had rolled back

on the sofa in pain. Then she had done a funny thing, he had thought later. While he was lying on his back, she had bent over him.

"I won't hit you again." Her voice had become suddenly excited.

Slowly, she kneeled on the floor in front of him, then came in over him, moving her body slowly up his until they were face to face. She pushed her hips against him, then withdrew, over and over, as if she were a man and he a woman. Excited again, he tried to take her clothes off, but she pushed him back and got up and started drinking her martini.

The whole scene had been eerie. He was both attracted to her and not attracted to her. He didn't know if she were a woman or a man.

It had taken Gene a little longer to get to know Faye Sherritt. In the few dates they had after Mark introduced them, she had hardly told him anything about herself, much less taken off any of her clothes for him. All he knew about her was that she worked in an office doing clerical work she didn't like, and that she was going to school at night, working toward a college degree. The biggest response he got out of her was once when he made some joking remark about Mickey. Faye immediately flared back at him.

"Mickey's all right," she snapped. "Leave her alone, she's all right. Just a little mixed up, that's all, leave her alone."

Sure, he'd leave her alone. He'd leave any woman who'd whack him the way she had, not to mention getting him excited and pushing him away *twice* in the same night. At least, he'd leave her alone until she changed.

Faye wouldn't let Gene pick her up at her home on the first few dates he'd had with her. He always had to meet her at a corner near her house. When he asked her why the corner meeting, she'd only mumbled something about her father being in a bad mood. And when Gene asked Mark for an explanation, Mark said, "She'll tell you when she's ready, Gene. She's very sensitive about her home life." Mark had known Faye for years.

About a week after Mark had introduced Gene and Faye, he invited them down to his house on Lake Michigan for coffee. Gene went to the usual corner to pick up Faye. She was waiting for him, reading a book. Tall for a woman, she wore a spring suit, which was buttoned tightly down the front, as if she were embarrassed by her jutting breasts. When she got in the car, Gene could see her panty line through the tight-fitting suit. She excited him just by sitting next to him, but he knew better than to try anything—yet.

Mark Kierson, dressed in an old sweater and ancient slacks, was at the door to greet them when they drove up to his house, a rented bungalow on the edge of the lake. Though it was not Gene's first visit to Mark's home, his gaze was stopped again by a painting on the living room wall, a modernistic thing, a picture of a Christlike head with large, luminous eyes; underneath the chin, as if coming out from the neck, a fist was knotted at the viewer. Mark had painted it.

Faye glanced at the painting, then quickly said, "That damn thing scares me, Mark."

"Thanks," Mark chuckled.

Mark went into the kitchen and came back with a monstrous pot and cups. He served coffee all around. The late spring sun had almost dipped into the lake now, and people were strolling along the beach next to Mark's house, watching and waiting for it to take its final sizzling plunge. At Mark's suggestion, they went out onto the front porch to watch, Mark taking along the coffee pot. At intervals, he poured himself and Faye and Gene cup after cup of the black liquid.

The phone rang and Mark went inside to answer it. He came back in a minute. "That was Mickey. She wanted to know who was here and as soon as I told her she said she'd be right down."

Faye's expression had gone rigid, Gene had noticed, when the phone rang. It seemed as if she had shifted her expression into neutral, as if she were trying not to show emotion. Yet Gene could see wiggling out of the neutrality an anticipation and at the same time something that looked like fear.

"Of course, you didn't tell her you'd be here tonight, did you," Mark said to Faye with a trace of sarcasm.

"No. She probably phoned home, and Mother told her where I was." Her voice tightened. "What's the matter, don't you like Mickey or something?"

"Oh, sure, I like her," Mark said. "But I know her, too. Known her a lot longer than you have. And I hardly think she's the best person in the world for you to get friendly with."

"Just what's wrong with Mickey, anyway? You act as if she's got worms."

"You know as well as I do what's wrong with her."

"Just because she's been married a few times doesn't mean anything."

"I'm not talking about her being married. You know what I mean."

"I don't know what you're talking about, Mark, and I don't think you do either."

Faye sulked then, her knees drawn in and up to her chin, her skirt tight around her hips and thighs, sipping coffee moodily as she sat next to Gene on a swing. She was still sulking when Mickey Jessup came walking up the street through the dusk. She walked in long loping strides, dressed in slacks and a turtle-neck sweater, hair cut short and combed straight, her lips now in a wide grin. She whistled in the gate and came onto the porch and sat down in the swing next to Faye, putting a brown paper sack she carried in her lap.

"Balls to the whole gawddam bunch of you," she muttered through her grin. "Why didn't you tell me you all were down here?"

"We thought sure you were busy with your minister buddies," Mark said.

"Oh, sure, sure. We spend the nights together all the time, soul-searching." She dug through her close-cropped dark hair with her unpainted fingernails. "I believe I got one here," she said, examining the tip of her finger. "Are you a soul?" she asked the tip.

Faye had pressed herself close to Gene when Mickey had sat next to her. She was tense; he could feel the muscles in her leg knotted hard against his.

"Let's go inside," Faye said. "It's getting cold out here." Before she had finished speaking she was up off the swing and going into the living room.

Mickey hesitated only a moment, then said, "Sure, let's go in. I need a drink anyway." She pulled a whiskey bottle out of the sack and gave it to Mark as she followed Faye. "Brought my own, of course. Otherwise, I'd be swilling coffee all night." She winked at Mark. "Gawddamn Kierson and his coffee. Bet you plant cans of the stuff in the spring, Mark, hoping it'll sprout."

Faye was sitting on the end of the sofa when Gene got inside, and, patting the seat beside her, motioned for him to sit there. But Mark was going for the kitchen with the bottle. "You want to help me with the drinks, Gene?" he said, and Gene followed him as Mickey, walking to the painting on the wall, said, "Hello, sweetie, have you missed me?"

"Faye, you want a drink?" Mark said.

"No, thanks."

As they made drinks in the large old-fashioned kitchen Mark said slowly in his soft voice, "I don't want you to get the idea I don't like Mickey, Gene. She's always welcome here, has been for years. We went to high school together, here in Chelsor." He handed Gene a drink. "She's a lot of fun, if you aren't too fancy about what you call fun. It's just that Mickey isn't good for Faye. And Faye has enough trouble with her father as it is." He started for the living room, then stopped and turned and said seriously, "I think a lot of Faye, Gene. We hope you do, too."

Gene reluctantly went back into the living room. He would have rather stayed awhile alone with Mark; it was a comfortable atmosphere when just the two of them were alone. He had the feeling it would be very nice to touch Mark.

Faye was sitting in the same spot on the sofa, her hand to her side saving a place for Gene. Mickey sat at the other end of the sofa. Mark gave her her drink and he refilled the coffee cups of Faye and Gene.

"Sure you don't want a drink, Faye?" Mark said.

She nodded no. She had been unusually quiet since Mickey had joined them on the front porch. Once Gene had seen her look quickly at the Christlike painting on the wall. But when Mark mentioned a book on psychology he was trying to get Faye to read, her interest seemed to quicken. Mark's question caught her unaware, though, and, sitting so close to her that they touched, Gene felt her stiffen.

"No." She forced a light laugh. "No, not me. I'm okay. I don't want to read any book on psychology. I'm okay," she repeated, as if she were trying to prove it to herself.

Mark said softly, "I know you're okay. It might be fun, though, to see what you have way down deep. Once in a while, you know, we can dig up something that's really charming and that we didn't know we were lucky enough to have."

"Balls," said Mickey.

"Then sometimes," Mark went on, his voice with a fatherly pitch, "we find out fouled-up things about ourselves that we can get rid of."

"I'm okay, nothing wrong with me," Faye said defensively.

"Oh, hell, Faye, nothing?" Mickey was grinning as she drained her glass. "Hell, I was hoping for something at least. Can't you dig up just a little wrong for Uncle Mark? Christ, there's gotta be something! What are you trying to do, act normal?"

Faye was smiling now; she had had time to relax. "Maybe I'm not as abnormal as you are, Mickey, but I'm trying."

"I've been trying to help you along, you know, but you insist upon going at your own slow speed," Mickey said.

Faye held her smile as long as she could; then it began to crumble and smear thin and its edges sagged. Her lips quivered and what she was going to say died in a weak, forced chuckle. Gene saw her knuckles whiten. In the silence a car could be heard going by outside.

Softly came Mark's voice: "What do you say, Faye, a little talk together sometime, just for the hell of it."

Faye's voice was a whisper. "No. No, Mark, I don't want to. But I'd like to read the book."

"I'll get it for you," he said.

He went to the bookshelf along the wall and got a book and gave it to Faye.

"Thanks." Without looking at it, she put the book beside her so that it was between her and Mickey. She got up quickly. "I'm going to fix myself a drink."

"I'll get it, Faye," Mark said. But she was going toward the kitchen.

"I need one, too," Mickey said as she got up and followed Faye.

Faye stopped when she heard Mickey's voice and realized that Mickey was coming into the kitchen, too. Faye turned and started back toward the living room, but Mickey took her by the arm and guided her to the kitchen.

With just the two of them in the kitchen, Mickey backed Faye against the sink, throwing her hips forward so that her body pressed into Faye. Quickly, Mickey put her arms around Faye and drew her into her arms, tight against her breasts.

Mickey's voice was sultry and intimate when she said, "What are you trying to do, baby, give me the runaround? You haven't been at my place for weeks."

"Mickey, please, don't talk about it here," Faye said. "I'll come see you later." She walked to the refrigerator for ice.

"You better had, if you know what's good for you. And you better lay off that poor sap, Gene."

When Faye came out of the kitchen by herself with a drink, Gene saw her walk toward the front door, then, confused, spin and go toward the sofa. Mark went rapidly into the kitchen, his face showing anger. Faye stopped before she sat down, and Gene saw her glance at the grotesque painting, as if she saw herself as also being grotesque. In the quiet Gene could hear Mark and Mickey talking angrily in the kitchen. Faye, at the sound, said, "I have to go!"

Mark and Mickey came back into the room, both unsmiling and tense.

"It's getting late," Faye said. "We better go."

"So soon, Faye?" Mickey's words were sarcastically light. "We haven't cut the marijuana yet. And we haven't taken a swim yet," she added. "It's just the night for it. No moon. No suits," she said for Gene's benefit. "We have a little swim club, Gene, that meets mainly on moonless nights and does clean-type things like swimming à la bare ass. But for some strange reason I don't think Miss Sherritt cares to tonight. Swim, that is."

"Come on, Gene, let's go," Faye insisted.

"We all do it, Gene," Mark said clarifying. "A whole group, mostly married couples."

"It's good for the soul," Mickey smiled.

"And for the skin," Mark said. "We always take some soap, Gene." He pulled a bar out of his pocket. "See?"

Faye was outside now and starting down the steps. Mickey followed her out onto the porch. Without waiting for Gene to open the door for her, Faye got into the car. He had started the auto when Mark called, "Wait a minute, Faye, you forgot your book!"

"Never mind, I'll get it later," she said. "Let's go," she murmured to Gene.

They hadn't gone more than a block when Faye was mumbling that she was very sorry about their sudden departure. "It's that damn Mickey," she said. "I wish Mark would make her stay away. She does the same thing with him that she used to do at my house—coming around all the time—until I told her to stop it. Or, I should say, my father told her. He and she used to go round and round until I thought sure he was going to strangle her. He almost did, for that matter."

As they were approaching Faye's home in Chelsor, she nervously lit a cigarette and from the choppy way she smoked it Gene knew she was tensed again. Her voice was strained and tight as she gave directions. They made a turn and were partially through a block when she said, "It's right in here." She peered anxiously out his side of the car. "Don't go too fast. I want to see if anybody's up." He could smell the faint musk of her perfume as she leaned over him to examine a house they were nearing. "Don't stop!" she said quickly. "Go on, go on!"

Gene pushed the gas. Two blocks further on she told him to turn, then said, "Okay, you can let me off here."

She leaned toward him for a kiss. Her arms went around him, her lips parted wide as he pulled her tightly against him. Her lips were softly sensuous; he had never felt such tender, yet passionate, lips against his. They seemed to draw him, to swallow him. Yet when he started to kiss her deeply, she closed her lips—reluctantly, it seemed to Gene. She still pushed herself tightly against him, though. He let his fingers drop slowly down her body to her ripe, round hips; she helped him, thrusting forward, as he pulled her in to him. Her large, full breasts grew firm as he bent to kiss them.

She moaned, "Oh, God, God—my body, it just wants and wants."

In the few dates they'd had, she had never been so excited as this when he had kissed her and tried to fondle her body. She had never let him do anything but kiss her lightly. She had not spread her lips for him before, and she had not let his hands go over her. On the other dates, though, they had not seen Mickey the same night; and Gene had a feeling that somehow Mickey was responsible—more than he was—for exciting Faye to the point she had reached now.

Faye suddenly thrust herself away, her head whirling toward the sidewalk. Gene looked up just in time to see a figure slinking away into the shadows of trees that bordered the street.

Faye quickly got out of the car. "Go on, Gene," she said urgently. "Don't stay around here."

"But there's someone under that tree."

"That's all right. I'm all right."

She turned and walked rapidly up an alley.

As Gene's car moved away from the curb, Faye stopped and looked back. In a few minutes she saw the figure enter the alley and start toward her. She quickly started to walk again, away from the shadowy form, breaking into a run when she saw that the figure was gaining on her.

"Faye, goddam it, stop!" the person yelled.

She was running hard when she reached the front porch of her house, a block away. The figure, a man, caught her on the top step.

"You little bitch!" he snapped. Liquor fumes hit her face. "Sneaking out, trying to sneak back in!" His hand cracked across her cheek. "You tell me before you go out, you hear!"

"I'll do as I please, Father!" Faye snapped back at him before she ran into the house.

CHAPTER THREE

The memory...the memory... Even from the beginning, even though he wasn't particularly overwhelmed by the seemingly mixed-up Faye, Gene was attracted to her. He thought it was merely curiosity at first, or because she started to refuse him dates and his ego was scratched, or because she was different—or because of that hot body of hers that she said kept wanting—men or women? He was determined to find out which.

He had rented a small apartment not far from Lake Michigan. It was nice to have a place of his own, the first time he'd ever lived in an apartment, the first time, too, he'd lived so far from home. It was also nice to have a place where he could take young Miss Sherritt—when she'd let him. He'd managed to get her on the living room sofa only once. They'd lain there together one night, taking deep kisses from each other, his hands searching her body under her clothes, feeling her quivering response. And she did more than respond. She became aggressive in their love-making. She pushed him down onto the sofa. Panting, her breath like fire, she had twisted him around so that she was above him. And he liked it this way; he liked to be somewhat passive and let her be the aggressor.

But she'd stopped him when he had tried to take off her panties and lead her into the bedroom. She stopped him at the last moment, throwing herself away from him, breathless.

"No," she said. "I'm a virgin. I must stay that way. It's the only thing I have left."

Gene didn't believe her. He'd learned a long time ago that most women who said they were virgins, weren't. He'd been fooled enough. But he'd play along with her.

"For Christ's sake, Faye, you can't stay a virgin all your life."

"I know, Gene," she said softly, "but I'm still staying a virgin. Like I just told you, it's the only thing I got left to hang onto in this damned mixed-up world."

After that night, she had refused to come to his apartment. And worse, she refused to see him, although she denied him nicely. Her no's were friendly, her negatives stroked him. She told him she had other things to do. She had a date, or she was going to school that night, or she had to wash her hair.

"Yeah, I know," he would say, a grin in his voice.

Or she told him she was going steady.

"Yeah? With whom?"

She laughed. "Oh, I'll think of somebody."

"I'll help," he said. "Let's go over the list."

They used small-talk chatter, soft-nothing words, which tingled back and forth over the wire. But the tingle always wore out when Gene, thinking he had worked her up to a yes, heard her again and again say no.

"Why?" he wanted to know.

"Now, Gene," she said as if he were a child—and which made him think of Mickey, for she treated him as a child, too—"I have a lot of things on my mind and always will, I guess, and there's no use you getting mixed up with them, and me, too. And I'll see you down at Mark and Pauline's every once in a while anyway. So what do you say?"

"What time will I see you tonight, that's what I say."

His phoning got to the point finally that he did it just for the hell of it. She never got mad, only a little disgusted with his persistence, which she let him know about in super-disgusted terms, and which Gene laughed about.

"My God, Gene, don't you ever give up? Is this your hobby? Or do you actually make money out of it?"

It was a game which he enjoyed and which, he sometimes thought, Faye enjoyed too. She laughed too many times as they talked, and often the tone of her voice told him she was glad to hear from him. And sometimes, too, when she said her usual no he thought she was sad about the no and about the reason for the no, whatever the real reason was.

Gene took the question of the real reason for her no to Mark one afternoon in the office after the paper was out and there was little for Mark to do. The city and society editors and two reporters were busy with their own work in the small editorial room, and they wouldn't bother Gene and Mark. Mark was editing wire copy when Gene pulled a chair up and sat down beside him and asked him quietly what was going on with Faye. But Mark was smilingly tight-lipped.

"Faye is a fine girl," he said. "You go after her."

"After her! My God, I've been after her for weeks now."

"Good. Keep it up."

"But damn it, Mark, why should I? And stop pushing me, will ya."

Mark grinned. "Why should you?—because Faye is young, attractive, intelligent, and a mystery. And because you're young you like attractive and intelligent girls and you like a mystery."

"Hm-m-m-m-m. I guess she's just my kind of gal, whatever that is," Gene murmured.

"Yeah?" Mark asked, serious and quick.

Gene, a little flustered by the direct, pointed tone of Mark's question, gave a halting laugh. "Oh, I don't know. She's just different, I guess. Not like the usual silly giggling girl."

"You mean she's not very girlish."

"Something like that. Maybe." He forced another laugh. "Oh, she's all girl, if that's what you mean. With that body of hers, she's solid woman. Well, I better get back to work," he said rapidly, with no break in his voice.

Gene went back to his desk feeling uneasily worried, just what about he couldn't pin down. Mark seemed to have some kind of special knowledge about him, and about Faye, too, for that much. He shrugged and hurried to lose himself in work.

But that afternoon he stopped often, and, unable to concentrate on his work, he stared out the window. Once Mark tapped him on the shoulder and murmured in his quiet, penetrating voice, "Stop dreaming about her and phone her—go after her." Gene felt a tremor shiver him. Had Mark been watching him all afternoon? And again he felt the urge to touch Mark.

The hell with it! He'd be damned if he'd keep phoning a girl who wouldn't respond. He never had before; the girl had to meet him halfway; usually, more than halfway; he liked to be chased; he liked to be asked.

So he stopped phoning her.

And she phoned him as soon as he stopped. She asked him, manlike, for a date.

"Meet you at your house, or down the street at the corner?" he asked her.

Uncertain, she finally said, "At my house. You've got to find out sometime."

That evening, before the early summer sun had gone down, Gene was at Faye's home, a squat wooden house with a porch that ran the length of the front and halfway around the left side. An uneven hedge enclosed the yard, and as Gene went up the walk his toe caught a piece of loose cement.

At his knock a small, thin woman with graying hair opened the door. She wore a faded dress with a sewing needle stuck in the front.

"Yes?" she said. Her voice was timid and hesitant.

"Is Faye here?"

"Why, yes, I think so."

A wan smile half-erased the woman's wary and worried expression. She stood in the doorway smiling absently at Gene, as if the mention of Faye's name was so pleasant to her that it made her hardly conscious of Gene waiting to be let in.

"I believe she's expecting me," he said.

"Oh, yes. Yes. Of course. Come on in, I'll call her. Faye!" she called as Gene went into the living room, "someone's here to see you!"

Chairs, two lamps, and a radio were in the coin-size living room. A rug, scuffed thin at the hall entrance, covered the floor. A man sat on a sofa.

"Have a seat," the woman said quietly. "Faye will be right down." She hurried to take a newspaper off a chair. "I'm Faye's mother." Then, quickly, almost reluctantly, as if she had to speak rapidly to get her words out, she said, her voice barely audible, "This is Mr. Sherritt."

Gene introduced himself and walked to the sofa to shake hands with Faye's father. The man watched Gene's approach with an inching, examining stare. A face that thinned, almost sharply, at both chin and nose smiling faintly at Gene, a slow weakening and sagging of his expression, forced and probing, as if it were ridiculously inappropriate for him to even smile at all. His eyes were a glittering wet. He slowly lifted his hand, and when Gene took it, it felt as if he had gripped a flopping-over banana skin.

"Hello," Mr. Sherritt said in a voice that was as faint as the dying end of an echo.

"If you'll just have a seat, Faye will be down in a minute." Mrs. Sherritt's words were jumpily quick now. Laughing nervously, she rubbed the palm of her hand down and up her side. "Faye!" she called again.

"I'm coming!" Faye answered with a snap in her voice.

"All right, dear, all right."

"You gonna take Faye out?" Mr. Sherritt said. He had the beginning of a sneer on his face.

"Yes."

"Now, Phil," Mrs. Sherritt said nervously.

"Watch her," the man said. "Watch her close." Unsteadily he got up from the sofa. He weaved once as he started toward what Gene thought was the kitchen. "You gotta watch her all the time, she's no good." He disappeared, and from the kitchen Gene heard the tinkle of glasses.

At the sound of the glasses, wrinkles sprouted under the eyes of Mrs. Sherritt. "Excuse me," she said as she hurried towards the kitchen. A loud rumble of voices came from the kitchen, and Gene was wishing Faye would hurry when he heard steps on the stairs and she was coming down to the living room.

Her flowing ebony hair fell in a soft glow onto the shoulders of the same suit she always wore. Because Mickey once commented that the suit was sexless, Gene examined it now more carefully. As far as he was concerned, it fit her as if it had been painted on. Just looking at her excited him. But he realized, too, that he had always preferred women who wore suits.

"Hello, Gene. Do you mind if my sister rides as far as the drugstore with us?"

"Course not."

Faye stepped to the stairs. "Hurry up, Bo!" she called. Turning to Gene, she said, "We might as well sit..."

A confusion of voices coming from the kitchen stopped Faye. Loudly came the slurred rumbling of Mr. Sherritt and the persistent squeak of his wife.

"Let's wait outside," Faye said, quick, urgent, nervous.

They went outside and in a few minutes a teenage girl burst out the door, her hair a red eruption. Her young ripe body was not as full as Faye's, but it was curved with perky breasts and a rounded bottom that jiggled deliciously.

"Gene, this is Bo, my sister, a dumbhead for sure," Faye laughed. "Bo, Gene Bond."

"Charmed," Bo giggled, doing an exaggerated curtsy. She looked at Gene and winked, then laughed; the sound was like the blast of a five o'clock whistle, short, clear, loud, exhilarating. Her face glowed with health.

They got into Gene's car and Bo gave Gene directions. The young girl, as they rode along, chattered on, her voice going like a machine gun, egged on by Faye's bursts of laughter and response as the blocks went by. Bo stopped Gene in front of a drugstore, and, chattering, she hopped out. She was still chattering when he drove away.

"How do you ever stop her when you can't get away from her?" Gene grinned.

"You don't. We have pillows at home we use, but she just chews them up and spits them out. Half the time I don't think she knows what she's saying. Or chewing."

Faye's laughter slid into a grin, and the grin into a memory-soft smile. "I used to be just like her," she said slowly. "A ball of fire."

"No more?"

Her head nodded in a quiet negative. "Sometimes I try to be, but it never works."

"Memories, memories," Gene hummed lightly.

"Yeah, if I don't watch myself, I live in them."

"Me, too. And sometimes they can be dangerous.

And they could be painful, he thought. Like the time when he was a kid and he had gone, alone, ice skating for the first time and some girls had hidden his shoes. He had cried his way home on suffering, limping, cold feet. His mother never would let him go ice skating again. And through the years his mother wouldn't let him do this, his mother wouldn't let him do that. She had never stopped telling him what he could and what he couldn't do.

Now, stopping at a corner for a light, Gene asked Faye to tell him, motherlike, where they were going that night.

"I know a pretty nice place. And it's not expensive. Called McIntyer's. I used to go there in the old days."

McIntyer's was a cubby-hole of a place, half underground, with a musical trio and a woman who crooned sexy numbers. An intimate spot. As Faye and Gene came in, groups of customers were paired at booths and tables in huddled conversation, their talk a low murmur behind the soft pulsations of the trio.

A few acquaintances greeted Faye as she walked to a wall booth. Faye nodded in return, and she and Gene sat down. As Gene started to sit down, he hesitated, stopped, wondering, peculiarly, whether to sit beside her or across from her, and at the same time wondered why he thought it important enough to wonder about at all. He sat across from her; it seemed more natural; he felt more at ease.

A waitress in a celery-crisp apron walked up to them and they ordered beer. When she brought the beer, Faye poured hers before Gene could pour it for her. Foam rushed to the top of the glass, and, as Gene watched, the tip of Faye's forefinger, slowly and absently, began to go around and around in the suds, her eyes a smoky wet as she stared at the bandstand.

Before they had finished drinking their first glass of beer a trio came onto the stand. Following them was a woman, her dress shimmering silverishly as it caught at the light behind the stand, holding her body in a sex-tight embrace as she stepped up to the mike, her breasts quivering as if ready to stand up and sing.

"Nice," Faye said. She twisted around toward the vocalist.

The woman began to sing, silkily, the words sliding out over layered lips, softly seductive, honeyed, her eyes and expression playing with the meaning of the words. Faye watched and listened intently, her beer forgotten, and when the number was finished her gaze came in a hesitant slowness back to Gene.

"Very nice," she said.

The trio slid into a crawling foxtrot. Couples edged onto the floor.

"Dance?" Gene asked.

"Later, if you don't mind."

She squeezed a smile into her voice. Gene watched the smile dissolve as she pulled her finger through the beer label, ripping the paper from the bottle. "Tell me something about yourself, Gene," she said. "Give me all the dope." A grin buckled her lips.

"Where do you want me to start, in the diaper stage?"

He told her, in quick capsule form, how he had been born and grown up in Virginia, not far from Rich-

mond, and gone to college in that city after he got out
of the service. He had worked one summer on a rural
weekly newspaper before he had come to Chelsor to
take a job as reporter on the *Press*. He told her his father had died when he was a kid and that his mother
had raised him. He skimmed over the details of his
mother; he didn't like to talk about her. He didn't tell
Faye that one of the reasons he left Virginia was to
get away from being babied by his mother. At least,
he told himself he wanted to get away from her baby-
ing. Sometimes, he had to admit, it was comforting.
Faye had the top button of her blouse undone, and
Gene could see the thrust of her breasts. Sometimes,
yes, being babied was comforting. And he was not
smiling when he thought it.

As soon as Gene stopped talking, Faye, her voice
embarrassed and painfully serious, said, "I want to
apologize for the way my father acted. Or for whatever he said."

"Forget it." He wanted to touch her arm, lightly,
tenderly, to let her know he understood and that the
understanding made things all right.

"That's why I didn't want you to come to the house
at first. Never know what Father is going to do or say.
He doesn't like men bringing me home. In fact, I can't
think of anything he does like. He's an alcoholic," she
said quickly. "He was drunk tonight, of course. How
he holds his job is beyond me.

"I hate him," she said quietly, levelly. "Sometimes I
hope he'll fall off a house he's working on. He's a car-
penter. Or supposed to be. Drunk all the time. Makes
life miserable for my mother. For my sisters. For me.
I just simply hate him."

Her hand was trembling now as she poured a glass of beer. Foam surged up and spilled over the side and Gene saw again the tip of her forefinger slop into the suds and start making slow, unconscious circular movements. Then, realizing what she was doing, she let her hand slide down the glass.

"Shall we change the subject?" She tried to smile; her forehead pretzeled into a mass of lines and grooves and wrinkles. "I mean," she finally grinned, "don't you think we better?"

"Talk about, if you want to," Gene said. "It might help."

"I've talked enough about it," she said. "But it does help sometimes to talk it out. To some people, that is." She grinned again, a beautiful healthy grin that erased her forehead wrinkles and made her face glow.

Lights dimmed in the club and a spotlight beamed blue in the cigarette smoke, and with the dimming of the lights Faye's grin, too, dimmed. She seemed to forget Gene and slowly, then abruptly, turned to the bandstand. The same woman vocalist stepped up onto the bandstand. Her body swayed softly against the mike, her smile caressing the audience as she began to sing, her words sex-puffed and honeyed. Dancers coupled onto the floor with the music.

"Dance?" Gene asked.

Faye unriveted her eyes from the singer and nodded, and walked with him out onto the floor.

"Stay away from the bandstand," she said. "The lights. I'm not dressed."

Yet they drifted out of the corner shadows, and Gene felt, peculiarly, that he was being edged toward the bandstand and the singer; and as he guided Faye back toward the darkened end of the floor, he was certain he felt her resistance, a stubborn submissiveness as he inched her into a dimly lit area.

"I thought you wanted to stay away from the lights," he chuckled.

He felt a tremor flash through her.

"I do."

Then she snuggled close to him, pressing herself in tight, pushing into him. "I do, Gene, I do. Keep me away from...there." She nodded toward the lighted area where the singer stood.

But within minutes he felt her again pushing into him, pushing against him until he wanted to take her outside into the car and the dark and into his arms. Pushing until they were again moving toward the bandstand. But her pressure stopped this time before Gene had to stiffen and guide her back; she seemed to realize suddenly what she had been doing; her resistance folded; she went warmly soft in his arms.

"Gene."

The word was pleading and soft. As Gene forced her from him, he saw that she was staring at the singer, intensely, as if both fascinated yet at the same time in despair.

"Do you know her?" he asked.

He felt her fingers digging into his back. "Let's go," she whispered, almost desperately urgent. "Let's get out of here."

Gene paid the check and they went out and got into the car.

"I never want to come back here again," she said as they drive away from the nightspot, her voice tired and empty now. "Never, never."

CHAPTER FOUR

Faye stayed slumped in the corner of the seat as they drove aimlessly away from McIntyer's. Gene felt like suggesting that they visit Mark. He thought a soothing talk by Mark might calm Faye and make her happy. Besides, he wanted to be near Mark too. He liked the feelings he had when he was around the older man—calm and soothing, yes, that was it, and restful. And the urge to touch Mark was increasing.

But Gene couldn't bring himself to suggest the visit without, first, asking, "Where do you want to go?" and, as he expected, Faye answered, "I don't care."

Lightly, too lightly, he said, "How about going down to Mark's?"

And as he expected, too, Faye's head whirled in quick no-spins.

"We wouldn't stay long," he said.

"How come you're so anxious to see Mark? Don't you see him enough at work? Does he have something I don't have?" She tried to prop lightness into her voice.

"He's a nice guy, that's all."

"That's all?"

"What do you mean?"

She shrugged and laughed. "Nothing. Forget it."

But Gene knew he wouldn't forget it. He never forgot anything that people said in relation to him when the words had a quality of mystery or suggestion about them, when their meaning was unclear. He was always afraid, too, of studying meanings too closely.

"Let's drive down by the lake," Faye suggested. "And I don't mean at Mark's."

"Okay."

At the lake, Gene drove into a parking area facing the water, and before he cut off the lights he let the beam rest a moment on the water.

"It's so peaceful," she murmured. "It must be wonderful to be like that—peaceful. Peaceful and strong."

Then, as he cut off the lights, he heard Faye let her breath roll out in a depressed and surrendering abruptness.

"Oh, Gene," she whispered. He watched her turn slowly to him. "Have you ever lost hope, Gene? All hope?"

"No," quietly.

"Believe me, it's the lowest, most bottomless feeling a person can have. To lose *all* hope—everything. Everything go up in smoke."

They could hear the waves of the lake caressing the shore with childlike slaps, intermittently, constantly, slapping against the background of their minds. The sound of the waves lulled Gene, so that as he sat in the car not knowing what to say, the sound of the waves mounted in the silence and seemed almost noisy as he stared at the silent Faye. He lit a cigarette. The smoke curled around her silence. He gave up searching in his thinking for conversation. He could think of absolutely nothing that would screw into the grooved threads of Faye's silence, nothing that would not bounce in gay nothingness and fall flat and incongruous in the vacuum.

"I'm sorry about what happened on the dance floor," she finally said. "Embarrassing you like that. It was the singer—something about her that scared me. It was her eyes, a certain way she looked at me, like she was a man after me, something like that. Like she was going to rape me. Her eyes looked like they had sweat in them."

Faye shuddered and Gene put his arms around her and drew her to him. There was no one else at the lake in their area; they had the privacy of a bedroom. His hand cupped her breast; the warm flesh seemed to melt into his fingers. Faye shivered and kissed his ear, then plunged her right hand in under his belt and let her fingers lie flat against his lower stomach. Both were breathing hard now.

"That singer makes me feel like this—sexy—just like Mickey did a few nights ago. Of course, you make me feel sexy too." She tried to chuckle, then took a long sigh and said, "You don't know what you're letting yourself in for, Gene, seeing me." Her tone was flat and deliberate within her heavy breathing.

"I'll take my chances."

"Why?"

He shrugged.

"Why do you want to keep seeing me?" she insisted. When he did not answer, she said, "You don't know, do you? You can't put it in words."

"The usual reasons."

"No, that's not it. No man wants to see me for the usual reasons. I know. Just like I don't want a man for the usual reasons."

"I like you, that's all," Gene said. "If you want me to tell you exactly why, the only thing I can say is that it's because of the usual reason a man likes a sharp-looking and intelligent woman."

"As Mickey would say, balls. No matter how sharp-looking and intelligent a woman is, no man likes her when she's as moody and unentertaining as I am."

"You'll change," he said. "You better had," he tried to chuckle.

"I doubt it. I've been this way for two or three years now. When I change it's not for long. Up and down, all the time. I'm on an emotional elevator."

"I like to ride elevators."

"Stop trying to be funny, Gene. Tell me the real reason you want to keep seeing me. If you don't tell me I'll find out anyway. I always do."

"Damn it, I told you."

Then she suddenly jerked and twisted in his arms so that she was facing him and he felt a slash of fear through him. He thought for a moment she was going to hit him. Her arm came up and went across his face. He drew back. But then her arm was around his neck and she was pulling him to her and kissing him tenderly hard, pressing herself to him. Pressing while her other arm coiled around his back and caressed and pulled. Her lips and body came to him, a hard-soft thrusting, a wanting, like a need that had been lost and wandering and had now found a road. Then her lips came down his neck and she clung to him for a moment before she pushed him back.

"Is that why you want to see me?" she said.

"Partially."

"I'm good at that. I can do that as well as any girl. You ought to know it by now."

"Better," he said. He started to pull her toward him but she kept back.

"Lots of times I don't want to, though. And I won't just because you want me to. Or expect me to."

"I know."

"I didn't want to particularly do it now. But I did to let you know I can. I can even do it better," she said. "But I don't play with doing it."

"I don't play just to be playing. It's got to be more."

"You wanted to just now. Play, that is."

"I wanted to and I didn't want to. Anyway, I did. Are you glad?"

"Yes."

She picked up his hand and held it. "I feel better," she said. "You make me feel good, Gene. You make me feel all woman."

He chuckled. "You make me feel all man."

"I told you I'd find out the real reason you want to keep seeing me."

Faye had chuckled, too, as she spoke; but the chuckle was lost in the meaning of the words. Underneath the chuckle the words stayed in memory, cold-sharp and clear.

Gene clung to her hand.

But she drew it away and said, "Let's go get something to eat."

After sandwiches at a diner, Gene, assuming that Faye wanted to go home, drove toward her house. She had not said a word for blocks when, as if she had been detached in thought and now suddenly realized they were nearing her home, she said, "I don't want to go home yet, Gene. Let's go over and see Mickey," elevating and lightening her voice when she mentioned Mickey as if to make her wanting to visit the church editor a joking matter of no actual importance.

"At this time of night?"

"She doesn't care. She's ready for anything anytime."

"I don't know," Gene said hesitantly.

"Oh, come on! Let's go!" The words jumped out of her in tense knots.

Gene reluctantly slowed the car and turned and started for Mickey's apartment. Faye lit a cigarette and smoked it in quick nervous puffs. They passed one car, then another. As they stopped for a traffic light, Gene glanced at her. Even in the slow glow of a street light her expression was granite-like; but the grin lost its props before it was built and it crumbled and left only a blank mask.

Gene went through the green light. Slowly, he shifted into second. He didn't want to go to Mickey's house, he didn't want to take Faye to see Mickey. He didn't care what time it was, he didn't want to go. He was afraid. He was afraid of something about Faye going there and seeing and being with Mickey. He was afraid of the feeling he had now, about the going there, about being there, about everything connected, whatever it was, about Faye and him and Mickey being together. Afraid. The way she, Faye, had brought it up, her voice so casual when she was not casual, so disinterested when she was not disinterested. He was afraid, and so was she. He ought to stop and turn around and take her home and tell her he wasn't going to take her to Mickey's.

But, instead, he shifted into third.

And drove on toward Mickey's, as if Faye were behind the wheel guiding him, telling him, showing him, ordering him. As if Faye was he, and he was Faye. As if she was the directing man, and he the passive woman.

Then she moved. She twisted in the seat. Her hand with the cigarette shot out and she plunged the butt in the ashtray, her voice jerking and breaking as she said:

"I don't want to go to Mickey's. Take me home, Gene. Please. Take me home now."

CHAPTER FIVE

No, Faye didn't go see Mickey that night, but she did later, on a night that Gene didn't know about. It happened after they—Gene and Faye—made a second night visit to the lake, about two weeks after their first visit.

The intervening two weeks had been disturbing ones for both of them. Gene, as he continued to see Faye night after night during those weeks, began to feel a strange fright toward her, a sinking feeling, a feeling that told him that by continuing to go out with Faye he was being slowly and relentlessly trapped. He would not phone her or meet her after school when this feeling came. He either sat by the phone in his apartment, afraid—yet at the same time hoping—that she would call, or he went to Mark's and did the same thing, for she would call him there. Or he went out and away from the phone and wandered, alone, feeling safe because she could not reach him, yet at the same time, within the same thought, unhappy within his safety.

The next time he'd see her she'd say, "Didn't see you after school the other night," her voice with just a trace of reproach, lifting the sentence from a mere statement of fact.

"No," Gene said. He felt a necessity to show his resistance with the word *no* and at the same time an urge to temper his denial of her with a smile, with a quick change of subject or a light "Did you miss me?"

She accepted and joined in with his levity. "Could hardly stand it," she purred.

She laughed, and everything was all right. Yet he was disturbed by her constant and quick acceptance of his resistance. Everything got all right too quickly, too easily. She shrugged off his no's with too little trouble, he thought, as if he were a speck in her soup which could always be dipped out.

"Did you *really* miss me, Faye?"

His voice, so suddenly serious, almost sad, drew her close to him; she opened herself and let him in.

"Yes."

Yet a cigarette later, after her smoking, thinking silence, she said:

"I want to be fair with you, Gene. Be straight." She let her fingers flick over his sleeve. "I don't know if I missed you or not."

His lips squeezed and he felt her hand on his arm tighten and dig into his skin.

"Oh, Gene, I don't know, I don't know, I'm not sure of anything."

But there was one thing she was sure of: that she hated her father.

"Meet me on the corner, will you, Gene?" she'd say over the phone, her words raspy with disgust and anger. "I got to get out of this house. Father's on a rampage again.

"I hate him, I hate him!" she said many times.

On these nights she wouldn't want to be "with people." She didn't want to go any place where she'd have to be sociable, particularly any place where she would be liable to meet friends or acquaintances, and especially where the people would be happy. On these nights happy crowds, she said, depressed her. And Gene, too, who once used to be fairly sociable, now found himself preferring activities that didn't require more than him and Faye.

Many times, though, Gene saw Faye's scorn of crowds merge with envy when she sat slumped on the periphery of a vibrantly alive group. Her expression sagging, she would try to shrug it off half-heartedly, then, failing, say: "What's the use."

She usually fell asleep going home at night in the car with Gene, something she did whenever the thing or things that were bothering her rubbed her sandpaperishly, and she wanted to forget. Gene would prod and shake and stir her with his voice until she was up and out of the car and into the house, or if a light was on in the living room, until she was out onto the corner nearest her home.

So by the end of a two-week period both of them were in need of a restful evening at the lake. They both—particularly Faye—seemed to take in the peace and strength of the water when their strange affair seemed to be getting both of them down.

They went to a section of the lake near Mark's house, a secluded spot, almost a private beach, overlooked by most swimmers because of its smallness. Mark, Mickey, Faye, and Gene, and their friends came here when they went to the beach, either in the night or day.

As they neared Mark's house, Gene asked, "Want to stop by and ask Mark if he wants to go with us?" Always he asked Faye; he never suggested on his own.

Faye gave him a curious look. "Mark?"

"Just thought we might ask him, since we're here and all." His voice was flimsy.

"No, Gene, not tonight, please. I don't feel particularly sociable after what just happened at home." Her father had cursed both her and Gene when Gene had picked her up earlier.

"Yeah, sure."

They drove by Mark's house and parked in the next block.

"What did you want Mark along for?" There was more than curiosity in Faye's words.

"I don't know. Just thought about him."

"When a man asks a girl to go to the beach with him, he doesn't usually ask a man along, especially at night."

She started to open the car door, then stopped. "Do you see Mark much, when I'm not with you?" Her voice was quick and sharp.

Slowly he said, "No. Just at work mainly," which wasn't altogether the truth. Quite often he came to Mark's house; but he realized now, with her question and his negative answer, that he didn't want Faye to know, and he wondered—almost worried—about the reason as he got out of the car and followed Faye over a dune and down an embankment to the lake's edge, below the level of the road and where they couldn't be seen by passersby.

Gene kept a beach blanket in the back of the car, and he carried it now to the beach and laid it out on the sand. He had felt uncomfortable since Faye's last question, and so he tried for the light touch as he said, "Crawl on." But Faye had slipped off her shoes and was walking down to the edge of the water and did not answer.

Gene went to her. They stood together and looked out over the lake. The moon was in the first quarter and they could see only a little way past the end of the breakwater pier that jutted out not far from where they stood. A cloud skitted in front of the moon and Gene tried to put his hand in Faye's but she pulled it back.

"What's the matter?"

"Nothing," she murmured.

He reached for her hand again and this time she didn't resist. It drooped passively in his, and Gene felt a sudden resentment at her and her disinterested hand. Since her insistent question and his weaklike answer he had felt a necessity to push himself against her, to show her that he, Gene Bond, was a man who took his women, or left them, as he pleased, and that he could take her now.

"Snap out of it," he said, trying to rough his voice so that she would know who was boss. But the words sounded ridiculously incongruous with the Gene that Faye knew.

She shrugged. "I can't. I can't fight something I can't see. I can't fight shadows." Her words were dry and flat.

"Get rid of the shadows. Make the shadows real. Mark said he could help you."

"I don't need Mark—you and your Mark."

"You need somebody. You can't handle this thing by yourself."

"Yes, I can. Give me time. I can straighten myself out. Give me time, that's all; just give me time."

"What's bothering you, Faye? Exactly?" He pushed from his mind what he thought it might be.

She hesitated, then blurted, "Oh, Gene, you must know, or at least suspect."

"No, I don't," he lied. He wanted her to give him a reason that would dispel his suspicions of her being attracted to Mickey, a lesbian. But she said the thing he most didn't want to hear.

"I like women in an abnormal way." Her voice was so low and sad that he thought she was going to cry. "I've been fighting it for years—sometimes the urge goes away, but it always comes back." He felt her fingers bite his palm. "That's why I'm depressed so much. Fighting this urge gets me down. I've never had physical contact with any woman, but I've come close to it a few times with Mickey."

She turned from the water and switched hands with him and led him back to the blanket. They lay on their backs gazing up at the acetylene-torch bursts of flickering stars, some dulled when an occasional wisp of cloud floated by.

"God, how I've changed," she said. A yearning was in her voice now, a resignation. "You should have seen me, say, five years ago, Gene, when I was the happiest person alive."

"I wish you were like that now."

"Now look at me—yearning after a woman. I've known Mickey for years. And what gets me is that I don't really—basically—like her." She shook her head despairingly. "But as long as I just want and don't touch maybe I'll win this damn battle."

"Maybe I can help," Gene said.

She put her hand into his. "You already are." Her voice was as soft as melted butter. "Just by staying around, even when I try to chase you away. But you realize now why I try to chase you away sometimes, don't you, Gene?"

He nodded.

"It's because I don't want to hurt you, like I've hurt so many other men."

"I'll take my chances," he said, pulling her close to him.

Then, quickly, she twisted her head and slid her open lips over him until she found his mouth. Her arms tightened around him in almost a clench, her body pressing down, twisting, squirming, rubbing her breasts like cushions that were in the way. "Faye," he was whispering, "Faye," one hand behind her neck and fingers brushing her ear, the other pressing into the boring small of her back. Her hand dropped down to his side, and he felt her fingers fumble on his hip.

She climbed on top of him. He put his hands on each buttock and pulled her tight against him. Then he tried to swing her off him, but she insisted on staying atop him. She was undoing his belt buckle when they heard someone coming down the beach behind them. They jerked apart and sat up.

In a loose, relaxed shuffle, the person walked toward them, alone and whistling gaily. As the intruder reached the level area and stopped and raised what looked like a bottle, Gene could see in the dim moonlight that it was a woman. "Wow!" the woman snorted as she lowered the bottle, and Faye started giggling,

"Who is it?" Gene whispered.

The woman started whistling again as she came toward the lake and their blanket, the bottle swinging at her side. She seemed to be reaching behind her back with the other hand as if she were loosening a halter strap.

"Mickey," Faye called, her voice tingling.

Mickey momentarily hesitated, then came toward them, her hand still busily fumbling with the strap behind her back. "Faye, doll," she chirped. "Who's that body beside you. Of course, it *is* a man," she added with a slight edge of sarcasm.

"It's Gene."

"Not Gene Bond, boy reporter, boy with the nose looking for nudes—or—news." She squatted beside Faye. "Here, undo this goddam strap, will you? They need some air." Faye reached to unbutton the halter strap. "Wait," Mickey said, drawing from her and turning back to Gene. "Gene, you do it. You need the practice, from what I can hear." Gene undid the straps and Mickey drew the halter over her head and tossed it to the side. "There," she breathed pleasantly, "that's so much better. My lit'le ole boobies have been whimpering to be put out all night."

Her breasts stood frankly proud in the cooling night air. "So," she said, "just what in the hell are you two doing here all alone? How do you expect to play checkers in the dark?"

Faye laughed. "You been up at Mark's?"

"In a way. I rapped on his door a wee bit ago with my martoonie bottle here, but he neglected to come to the door. So I went in, went in the bedroom, and there Mark and a woman were, guilty as hell, in bed together. I offered them a drink, which they refused, told them I wouldn't tell, then came down here, Do you want a drink?" she said, swinging the bottle toward them. "It a well-prepared mixture of gin and vermouth, shooken well, I might add."

Faye didn't take any, but Gene tried the drink, gasping as he handed the bottle back to Mickey.

"Good, eh," she snickered. She swilled a swallow, going, "Woo-o-o. Delicious," she intoned. "Well," she said, standing up, "you two going to lie there all night doing those *things* or are you gonna take a dip with me?" She was taking off her shorts and blouse.

"You want to?" Gene asked Faye.

Faye was watching Mickey step out of her panties. Gene could smell her nakedness—musky, fleshy.

"Well, do you?" Mickey turned toward Faye as she spoke, profiled for Faye against the sliced globe of the moon. Then she squatted down.

Faye gave an artificial laugh that scraped against her nervousness. "No. No, I don't think so."

"Aw, come on," Mickey said with exaggerated emphasis.

"Some other time," Faye said.

"Always later. Always putting things off. Balls," she said. She stood and turned toward the water, then stopped. "How 'bout you, Gene?"

"I'll watch."

"No fun watching," she chuckled. "Is it, Faye?" she emphasized.

She went into the water then with a running drive, came up burring and wowing while Gene and Faye watched her from the blanket. Faye had put her hand in Gene's now, and as she watched Mickey, Gene felt her fingers tighten around his.

"Give me the bottle," she said.

Gene handed her the mixture. She drank, the liquid gurgling, then drank again and handed it back to Gene as her hand went again into his, fumbling, pressing, gripping, hunting him, holding him, needing him, keeping him close to her while Mickey splashed alone and away.

"What a character," Gene murmured.

But Fay did not answer.

Dripping, Mickey splashed out of the water. She came to the blanket and wiped herself with hands. "Forgot to bring a towel. Move over, Faye."

Faye wiggled closer to Gene, still holding his hand, and Mickey flopped on her stomach down beside them, next to Faye.

"We got to go in a minute," Faye said.

"Really? Why, the checker game over?"

"It's late," Fay mumbled.

"It's not light yet. I think I'll stay here all night." She turned her head lazily toward Faye. "All night," she murmured casually.

Faye sat up. "Let's go, Gene. You don't mind if Mickey keeps the blanket, do you?"

Gene said no and got up with Faye, who was already standing a few feet away from Mickey.

"I'll bring the blanket to you," Mickey said to Faye. "You can give it to Gene."

"No. Give it to Gene at work."

Mickey shrugged and turned over on her back and looked up at Faye. Outlined by the moon, she was a naked invitation. "Whatever you say, doll," she drawled, honeyed and amused. "Say hello to sister Bo for me."

Faye and Gene said goodnight and they went up the bank and got into the car. Just before Gene pulled away they heard Mickey begin to whistle; it was a lonely and empty sound.

On their way home Faye sat close to Gene, the first time she had done this while they were driving. Her nearness was strangely awkward to Gene; there was something incongruous about her sitting so close to him in a moving car as other girls did and had done. With other girls, it seemed natural; with Faye, it didn't. Faye seemed to sense this incongruity, too, for she soon moved away from him to her own side of the seat, murmuring apologetically that she didn't "feel comfortable." She stared out of the window, letting her head rest against the back of the seat.

"Want to get something to eat?" he asked, more to make conversation than anything. Their quiet bothered him.

"You can. I'm not hungry."

"I can wait."

They drove through blocks of noisy silence, loud in Gene's consciousness. Faye was slumped into the corner of the seat. "If only I didn't have a body," she finally said. "A body that wants and wants..." her voice tore "...and wants!"

Gene wanted to put his arms around her and draw her close, make room for her inside of him for her hurt to be sheltered in. But when he put his arm out to bring her in to him, gently and tender, she stiffened and wouldn't come and went away with herself, alone.

When he stopped in front of her home a light in the living room was on, but Faye did not tell him to drive on to the corner so he stopped in front. As they walked to the door she put her arm around him and fitted herself to his stride, her hand holding his again.

"I'm sorry," she said.

A breeze caught at her hair; a strand brushed his chin. Her face was tenderly sad, and Gene wanted to cup it in his hands and kiss it and make it smile for him. Her smile could be so beautiful; by itself it could make him sing.

"I know it's getting to be a habit," she said, "apologizing to you." She tightened her arms around him and kissed him. "Oh, Gene, you're so good to me."

She turned quickly and opened the door and went in.

As Gene walked back to his car a light in an upstairs window flashed on. He mechanically looked up and saw Faye and her father, their arms whirling and jerking in argument. The window was partially open. Gene heard Faye shout:

"Get out!"

"You bitch!" her father yelled.

Gene could hear the door slam as Mr. Sherritt left Faye's bedroom.

CHAPTER SIX

Gene got into his car and started back to his apartment. But en route he began to think of Mickey lying naked on the beach at the lake. The more he thought of her, the hotter he felt. He remembered the evening he had spent at her apartment, when she had taken off her clothes down to the waist and rubbed her firm breasts over him. Even if she had not taken him to bed, she had made both of them hot.

The more he thought of her, the more he wanted her. Besides, Faye had been exciting him so much the last few weeks, without going to bed with him, that he was about to burst. He needed a woman. And right now, even if it was Mickey. Of course, maybe she'd only frustrate him as she had done before, but he'd chance it. He had smelled her earlier at the lake; now he wanted her. He'd sink his teeth into that nice body of hers until she'd beg for him. Maybe she wasn't all woman psychologically, but she was enough woman for him physically. Besides, if he could satisfy her maybe she would leave Faye alone.

He turned off his homeward route and drove toward the part of the lake where he and Faye had just left Mickey. He parked the car in a side street about a block from the beach so it wouldn't be seen at the lakefront; he didn't want visitors while he was with

Mickey. When he got to the sand, Mickey was still lying on the blanket, naked and softly humming.

"Doll," she said, "welcome back. Little ol' me has been saving a place for you—or Faye." She patted the blanket beside her. "Lie down and have a drink—on me," she chuckled.

Gene took off his shoes and lay beside her, then took a drink out of the bottle. The moon caressed her nakedness. And he could smell her so strongly that his heart began to bang. "I took Faye home," he mumbled. His voice was shaky.

"So I figured," Mickey drawled. "I didn't think you had her with you. Unless you left her back there on the bank to watch us. That's the only way she gets any these days, as far as I know—watching. Helluva thing," she snorted, taking another drink. "Me, now, I'm strictly a do-it gal.

"Doll," she chuckled, "do you want some of little ol' me? I'm hot tonight."

"It would be nice."

"Maybe it would, maybe it wouldn't. I'm rough. I just don't lie on my fanny like other girls do and get bounced on, like I'm a mattress or something."

"I'm willing to play the mattress bit," Gene murmured. "Just you go right ahead."

"You'd be nice for a change, doll."

"What do you mean?"

"Why, doll, you know what I mean. You're a man, or part of one, anyway. Me, now I ordinarily like womenfolk. But fortunately for you," she sighed, "I like *both* women and men sometimes. It's nice this way. I got twice as many to choose from."

"Always doubleheaders, huh."

"No. I'm a one-at-a-time gal. One a night, that is. Either sex. Or half-and-half sex, like with all my husbands, and you, for example."

"Half-and-half, hell!" he snorted, sitting up and pushing her to the side. "I'm all man."

"Balls. You're just like my husbands—half man, half woman. That's why I married 'em. I like both, remember. That's why I'm getting ready to take you on. You got enough woman in you to excite me."

Then quickly she pushed him back onto the blanket and lay half on him. "Relax now, I won't hurt you," she said, her voice rising in passion. She pulled up his shirt and sat on his stomach, her legs on either side of him. Then she began to raise and lower herself, like Faye had done, still staying in the sitting position on his stomach, not letting him push her down onto the blanket. She began to hum, only stopping the sound to take a drink. She even offered him a drink. He declined.

"Damn it, Mickey, let's have some action."

She gave him a throaty chuckle. "I'm just oiling out the kinks, Gene boy."

She took one more drink, and with the gin still burning her tongue she suddenly slid down onto him. He tried to push her over on her back, but she said, "No, we'll do it my way." She stayed on him when he had taken off his clothes, bouncing over him with powerful manlike pushes of her body. Her hand reached behind him, holding him close in to her, as he had done so many times with women. She began to groan, noisy panting sounds, and her body movements became frenzied until finally she gave almost a scream. She collapsed on the blanket and lay quietly panting.

"Goddam," she finally said, "I'm pooped. Hand me that bottle, will you, boy?"

Gene gave her the bottle, rested a few minutes, then got dressed and went back to his car. Just as he was opening the door, he saw a taxi go by on the road that led to the spot where Mickey was. He could see a woman's head in the back seat of the cab, and as the taxi went under a street light he recognized the woman as Faye. Something in his belly did a flip flop.

His stomach balled into a knot of fear and jealousy when he realized that Faye was going to see Mickey on the beach. Quickly he closed the car door and walked down to the lakeside street in time to see the taxi stop at the beach where Mickey was. Faye got out of it and went down the bank to the water. Gene walked quietly up the street and crept onto the sand at a point about seventy-five yards from where he had left Mickey. He took off his shoes and began to tiptoe slowly toward the blanket. When he could hear the voices of Mickey and Faye, he dropped to his knees and crawled slowly toward them.

"Then why did you come?" he heard Mickey say.

"I was lonely," Faye answered.

"Balls. You want the same thing that I do. We're the same."

"No, we're not." But Faye's voice was hesitant and unsure.

Gene crept quietly to a mound of sand only a few yards from the blanket. He could easily see the two women in the moonlight, and he was hidden from them behind the pile of sand. They were sitting close to each other, Mickey still naked, Faye fully clothed.

"You're over the fence," Faye said, "and I'm still fighting it. And I always will," she added defiantly.

Mickey chuckled sarcastically. "Then you shouldn't come here to see me." Gene saw her lightly caress Faye's hair. "Because, honey, I'm going to bring you over to my side of the fence. I'm going to make a lesbian out of you if it kills both of us."

"No, you're not. I just have tendencies, that's all. I can control them."

"Take off your clothes and say that," Mickey snorted.

"Al right. I'll show you."

Gene saw Faye stand up and slip out of her skirt and blouse. He gasped when she took off her bra and panties. He had never seen her naked. Under the moon, she was an earthly slab of heaven. She stood above Mickey, her full, proud breasts winking down at the woman, her ripe body, rich with curves, glistening whitely in the moonlight. Gene could hardly control himself.

"Very nice," Mickey murmured as she gazed at Faye.

"Okay," Faye said challengingly, "I got my clothes off, what are you going to do about it?"

"Oh, nothing, child, nothing." Mickey grinned. She nonchalantly let her fingers glide up Faye's leg.

"That doesn't bother me."

"Does this?"

Mickey's hand went on up the inside of Faye's thigh.

"Not at all." But Faye's voice was shaky.

"You sure, doll?"

Then Mickey stood up beside Faye. Her arm went around Faye, and Gene saw their bodies merge as they kissed passionately. "Doll, doll," Mickey murmured huskily. Both hands slipped behind Faye's moonlit buttocks, and she pulled Faye close to her, arching her back as if she were a man.

Gene, excitement shooting through him like an electric current, heard Faye moan, "Oh, God, oh." But when Mickey tried to take her down onto the blanket, she pushed away. "No," she groaned. "No, I won't do it." Then before Mickey could stop her, Faye snatched up her clothes and ran up the bank.

CHAPTER SEVEN

A sliver of light peeped from beneath the shade of Mickey's ground-floor apartment as Gene walked toward her front door. The *Press* had sent him out to cover a lodge dinner that night, an affair that had boasted of steaks and a somewhat renowned speaker imported from Chicago. The steaks had been raw and the speaker, as far as Gene concerned, was more than well-done; he was finished. Gene had chewed his way through part of a steak and digested part of the speech, had written his news story, and now, before going home, had left his car at the *Press* and walked the short distance to Mickey's apartment to pick up his blanket, which she had forgotten to bring to him at work that morning. He had tried to phone her at first, but her line remained busy.

Of course, he wasn't coming around just to get his blanket. After last night on the beach with Mickey, he was as hot as a firing machine gun. He'd been hot all day thinking about what had happened on the beach, both between him and Mickey and between Mickey and Faye. Mickey hadn't shown up at work; she'd phoned in and told the managing editor she was sick. Sick, hell, she was exhausted, Gene figured, after taking on both him and Faye, although Faye had left before Mickey could go all the way. But Gene had sat behind the hump of sand, after Faye had gone, and watched Mickey for a long time.

Gene was proud and sad about Faye's conduct on the beach. He was proud that she had not given in to Mickey but sad that she had been attracted enough to come to the beach in the first place. The incident reminded him of the time when he had caught her and a guy in the guy's apartment.

Faye had phoned him a couple of weeks or so ago and asked him to come and meet a friend of hers, a man whose apartment she was phoning from. "He's a real character!" she had zipped. "A nut!"

Lew Phinney was a character all right, a nut, and he was also extremely handsome, a fact that Faye had neglected to point out when she phoned. Too handsome. Hollywood-type handsome. There was something phony about the guy, and right away Gene didn't like him. He was a slick character, full of sarcasm and oil, dressed to the teeth, manicured nails flicking his cigarette so goddam precisely, his ultra-cultured voice rounding and timing his words so exactly, his wavy hair with just the correct amount of gray at the temple. He had Faye rolling over lazily in the palm of his pink hand.

And there was another reason why Gene didn't like Phinney. When Gene had arrived at the apartment that night, the door was open, so Gene had walked on in. The first thing he saw was this slick Phinney with his hand up Faye's dress. She was drunk and so was he. Faye's dress was up above her black panties. But what killed Gene was that they were laughing about the whole thing. As Phinney snapped Faye's panties, they laughed like hell at the sound. Even when they saw Gene, they kept on laughing, although Faye did manage to get her dress down.

"Would you *please* pull off that sock" were the first words Gene heard Phinney say, his goddam foot stuck up at Gene.

Faye thought that was funny as hell. So Gene let her pull off the sock.

"Quite a dump you got here," Gene let him know.

"Admittedly," the man said. "The woman I'm living with—but whom I utterly *despise*, believe me—thinks it's rather charming herself. She owns it, you see. Of course, she's rather old and it doesn't *really* matter," and the cutie spun a filtered smile through his too-perfect teeth at Faye, who laughed and laughed. Gad! was this man funny!

This sort of junk went on for a couple of hours before Gene finally managed to get Faye out of the apartment. Phinney had her drunk by the time Gene got there, and he kept feeding more alcohol to her, and to Gene, too, and to himself, all the time going on with his phony chatter and sarcasm prancing around the apartment, flinging his arms all over the place. Gene thought he had had just about enough when he went to the bathroom and came back and found the queer and Faye doing some kind of dance; she was jumping into his arms, he was jumping into hers. Then they both went bang on the floor and laughed and laughed and laughed.

Faye surprised Gene by coming with him and leaving Phinney when Gene suggested it. Phinney didn't seem to mind that Gene was taking Faye out of his little playhouse. In fact, Phinney seemed glad to see Gene when he came in. Funny thing, Gene thought;

in an apartment by himself with a knockout like Faye, she drunk, and he greets the visitor as if it were old-brother week. Outside, going down in the elevator, Gene mentioned this peculiarity to Faye.

"Nothing peculiar about that as far as Lew's concerned," she said, smiling. "That's normal behavior with him. In fact, he asked me to call you and invite you over."

"One of the limp-wrist boys, huh?"

"Sure. Couldn't you tell?"

"Wasn't sure," Gene said. He was sure from the beginning, but he didn't want to admit it to himself.

Now, standing in front of Mickey's apartment, just thinking about that night made him mad. Yet, it also excited him a little, just like thinking about last night on the beach excited him a lot. He had always got very excited the times he'd seen sex action. He'd looked through many a bedroom window in his life, and he'd seen all kinds. Watching excited him as much as doing it himself.

So when he saw the sliver of light coming from under Mickey's apartment window shade and remembered watching her and Faye on the beach the night before, he went to the ground-level window and looked inside.

At first he saw no one in the living room. He heard only the record player; it was playing a soft, seductive number. Then he heard feminine voices, and a movement to one side of the room made him turn his gaze to the right. What he saw shook him down to his guts.

Bo, Faye's teenage sister, was taking off her clothes for Mickey. Facing the window, Bo had her back to

Mickey. Mickey's eyes were watching her hungrily as Bo pulled her dress over her head; the older woman's tongue licked around her lips as Bo undid her bra strap. Then a ball of desire rolled over Gene. Bo stepped out of her panties and stood in lovely naked innocence not ten feet from Gene.

"Oh, you're beautiful," Mickey said in a husky voice, a voice that Gene knew was filled with sexual hunger.

Bo blushed. She looked down at her young, proud breasts, rose-colored at the tips; at her firm, curvy body with golden flesh. She was a virgin beauty. She kept her back to Mickey; all her untouched loveliness faced Gene. With aching desire, he wanted to press her ripe body against his.

Mickey stayed a few feet behind Bo, her eyes hungrily devouring the younger girl. She seemed to be fighting almost an overpowering urge to take Bo in her arms and cover her body with kisses.

"Will you hand me the suit?" Bo asked, ignorant of Mickey's desires.

Mickey took a bathing suit from a chair beside her and gave it to Bo. Her hand lay only for a moment on the girl's cream-colored back before she withdrew it.

Bo got into the suit. "Gee, Mickey, it sure was nice of you to get me this for my birthday. It must have cost you a lot."

The suit fit on her so tightly it looked as if it had been ironed on. The dainty pillows of her buttocks rippled invitingly as she turned to Mickey.

"You're a good kid," Mickey said huskily. Her eyes gleamed damply at the desirable girl. She took Bo in her arms and gave her what Bo thought was a sisterly hug. But she held the younger girl too tightly and too long, and Gene knew that Mickey could hardly control herself. Gene saw Mickey's hand start down Bo's body in a caress, then stop. She reluctantly let Faye's sister step back from the embrace.

"Gee, I can hardly wait to show it to Hal."

"Who's Hal, doll?"

"My boyfriend."

"Watch out for boys, doll. They're men, you know, even if they're young, and they can get you in a lot of trouble."

Bo blushed. "Not Hal. He wouldn't do anything like that. And I wouldn't let him, either."

Mickey laughed huskily. "That's what you think. The only thing a boy thinks about is taking his girl to bed. Then, of course, she gets pregnant. The boy doesn't care."

Bo had turned her back to Mickey and was starting to take off the bathing suit. "I wouldn't do anything like that," she said firmly.

She was having trouble getting the tight bathing suit down over her full hips. Mickey stepped close to her. "Let me help you, doll." She put her palms on Bo's waist, so that the ends of her fingertips were near the girl's belly button. Then, slowly, very slowly, Mickey began to work the bathing suit down the girl's hips.

"You'll never be a woman until you have sex, doll." Mickey was so excited that she could hardly control her voice. "But a man will make you pregnant." Her fingers were now slowly caressing the young girl's body.

Gene saw that although Bo's expression was bewildered, it was also beginning to fill with pleasure. He realized that if he didn't stop Mickey she was going to make a lesbian out of the innocent girl. He was torn between the desire to keep on watching the scene and saving the girl. With all the willpower he could muster, he quickly turned from the window and ran to Mickey's front door.

When he rapped sharply, someone inside turned off the record player. He heard quick footsteps squeaking the floor. Then, silence. He rapped again, and waited, hearing nothing.

"Well, aren't you going to answer the door?" he heard Bo say.

He rapped again, louder. "Okay, come on, open up in there!"

"Gene!" He heard the scramble of hurrying feet. The door shot open. In the doorway, a grin bursting her face into a pink blossom, stood Faye's sister. She had pulled the bathing suit up over her shoulders. She looked like a sexpot—in a clean, refreshing sort of way. Gene wanted to take her to bed himself. "Enter, sir," she grinned, although Gene could tell she was nervous. "We ladies await your pleasure."

Gene went in. Mickey's studio apartment was done with almost masculine taste. The couch was leather-ish, the curtains were heavy and drape-like; the place had not a flower or plant in it, and through an opened closet door Gene could see the many pairs of Mickey's slacks. The only things missing were pipes and slippers, and maybe a pool table. Bo's clothes were on a chair.

Mickey, holding a drink, stood fumbling with the record player. Her usual good-humored smirk was absent; she was jittery and confused as she snapped on the player and walked too quickly, her motions nervous and snaplike, toward him, her voice coming through a strain as she said, "I know what you want, the blanket, now where did I put it." She went to a heavy dark bureau and rummaged through bottom drawers, then, almost spinning, turned and strode to the closet, where she found the blanket on an upper shelf and brought it to him. "Still sandy," she managed to grin.

"I always use sand," Gene said. "No toothbrush."

Bo giggled away her nervousness. "Oh, Gene," she said.

"Oh, Bo," he said.

"Where's that sister of mine?" she asked.

"I don't know. I had to work tonight. I haven't talked to her since yesterday."

"Fine thing," Mickey murmured. "You gotta do better than that with Miss Sherritt."

"Gene will," Bo let him know. "In fact, he does. I know 'cause I listen to Faye talking in her sleep. Wow!" she laughed.

Mickey stiffened. "Faye doesn't talk in her sleep."

"All the time."

"You're kidding."

"Goes on for hours," Bo said. "Even when she's awake she talks in her sleep."

Mickey relaxed, understanding now that Bo was joking. "You're a nut." She laid a momentary hand on Bo's arm, then withdrew it. "Bo and I accidentally bumped into each other tonight," she said to Gene quickly, too quickly, as if she felt it terribly necessary to explain Bo's presence.

"Yeah?" Gene said. He didn't believe her.

"I came out of a show and there Mickey was," Bo explained. "See what she got me for my birthday." Bo twirled, showing off the bathing suit.

"Good for her," Gene said dryly.

Bo picked up her clothes from the chair and went into the bathroom. Mickey fixed Gene a drink, then sat on the sofa beside him, lit a cigarette, and eyed him with her veiled and amused sarcastic look.

"Little Boy Bond," she murmured, "out in the night looking for his blanket. I suppose you and Faye are going to go roll in it tonight. Where is she, anyway, out in the car? Why don't you ask her to come up? Doesn't she like my company anymore?"

"I haven't seen her since last night."

"How can you stand it."

"I just suffer through."

"Lay off her, doll. She can only hurt you—and if she doesn't, I will."

Bo came back from the bathroom and said, since it was late, that she had to leave. She was putting on a light coat when someone knocked on the door. Bo kept putting on her coat, but Mickey, who had raised her drink to her lips when the knock came, stopped; she tensed, holding her drink halfway to her mouth. Then, reluctantly, shrugging, she went to the door.

"Who you been talking to all this time?" Faye said, a grouch in her voice as she came in. "I been trying to get you for hours." Without looking to her right and into the part of the apartment where Gene and Bo were, she swung to her left toward the phone, which sat on a stand in the kitchen entryway. "Just as I thought. The phone's off the hook."

"Huh, that's funny," Mickey murmured.

"Funny, hell. You took the receiver off on purpose. Who..." Breaking off her words, Faye swung around and saw Gene and Bo. Her eyes flashed back to Mickey. "What are you trying to do?" The words were meant for only Mickey to hear, but the grating sound carried to Gene.

"I just came over to get my blanket," Gene found himself saying, as if he had to make an excuse for his presence at Mickey's apartment.

"Bo," Faye said, the word sandpapered with worry, "it's late. You better be going home."

"Okay." Bo's grin was gone. "Look what Mickey gave me for my birthday," she said quickly, too quickly. She held out the suit for Faye to see. Faye ignored it.

"I'll take you," Gene said. "You coming, Faye?" He felt a weakening, an emotional skidding at the question; why didn't he tell her, too, that he was taking her home? Why wasn't he a man about it!

She nodded and turned to Mickey, glaring at her.

"What's the hurry?" Mickey wanted to know. "This is ol' company night, and now everybody's rushing off. The place isn't on fire, you know." Mickey was trying to be casually calm; but the casualness was destroyed by Faye's glare. "Dammit, Faye," she finally said, "what are you staring at!"

"Nothing. Absolutely nothing." Faye started toward the door. "Let's go."

Mickey followed them to the door. As they were going out, she said coldly, "By the way, Faye, what was it you were phoning me about?"

Faye ignored the question, and the three of them walked silently to the *Press* and got Gene's car and started toward Bo and Faye's home.

"Don't you ever go up to Mickey's apartment again, Bo," Faye said after blocks of quiet.

"Okay."

"She's too old for you to be fooling around with."

"She doesn't seem old. She acts my age."

"Yeah, I know."

"She's friendly, too. Whenever I see her she asks me to come up to her place."

"Well, don't do it. She's a phony. Stay away from her."

"Is something wrong with her?" Bo asked.

"She's just different, that's all. But she's a phony, too."

"She keeps talking about wanting to take me to someplace between here and Chicago."

Faye's head spun toward her sister. "What's the name of it?" she said quickly, worriedly.

"The Intimate, I think she called it. She says she goes there a lot. She said I'd like it."

Slowly, precisely, restraining the urgency, Faye said, "Bo, don't you ever go any place with Mickey, you hear me. Especially that place she mentioned."

"It must be really a place."

"Never mind. Just don't go there."

"I won't," Bo said, disappointed.

They drove up in front of the house and Bo got out and started inside. A light shone from the living room

"Go right upstairs," Faye said. "I'll be in in a few minutes."

"I will. Goodnight. Goodnight, Gene. Thanks for the ride home."

Gene told Bo goodnight and she went inside.

"She's a good kid," he said.

Faye nodded. "Too good. People take advantage of her. Like Mickey. She's after Bo now, instead of me."

Faye's lips were tight now, and wrinkles grooved her forehead.

"I better go in," she said quietly. She got out of the car. Together they walked to her door.

"Gene," she said, "are you sure you want to keep seeing me?"

"Of course I'm sure."

"It might be better for you—for me—if we called it quits. I can hurt you. I've done it to other guys. Good guys, like you."

"You aren't hurting me."

"I've never wanted to, but it's always happened. Before."

"It's not going to happen now."

"I hope so," she said. "For both of us. I hope so. You're sure, Gene? That you—want me?"

"Very much."

Then she was kissing him, holding him, pressing her body into his.

"Gene," she said. "Oh, Gene, don't go away. Don't leave me like everybody else."

"I'm not going any place."

"Oh, Gene. Please don't. Please. I need you, Gene. I need you bad. Sweet Gene," she said.

"Let's go back out in the car. Let's go someplace."

"No," she said. "But we will. We'll go someplace just the two of us. My Gene," she said. "You're so good to me. My Gene. I like the sound of the words. My Gene."

CHAPTER EIGHT

Faye laughed. Her face was toothpaste-fresh on the shadowy side of the car, bright and warm as the summer sun on Gene's arm elbowed out the side window. They were driving to an inland lake over an old asphalt road, Gene taking the dips and bends almost recklessly, exuberantly, with a new Faye, a daytime Faye, an alive Faye.

Saturday afternoon. Just Faye and a Saturday afternoon, a Faye who, looking out the window at a coltish horse they passed as it kicked tuffs of earth skyward, said, animated and flushed, "It's so good to be living, Gene," so different from the usually depressed Faye. By herself she seemed to have changed—at least for the moment.

Reaching the lake, they stopped at Faye's suggestion and went into a building that jutted out over the water, a barnlike structure with a bar running the length of one end and the rest of the interior sardined with tables. Behind a dance floor in the middle of the building, on a low platform, was a five-piece jazz band bursting and wailing in musical explosions.

At the sound of the music, Gene felt Faye's fingers suddenly grip his arm. She led him to an empty table, hurrying, sitting down quickly, and turning to the band, almost rigidly, her body now moving rhythmically, undulating with the wailing jazz. Her hands tapped on the table, keeping the beat as the trumpet-man cracked a note, pulled the note from the air and sent it shooting through the roof.

"O-o-o-o-o," she gasped.

A fat waitress with a soiled apron waddled up to them. Gene ordered two beers, and the waitress departed.

The dance floor was a wiggly mass, dancers smoothly jerking to the sharp-edged music like oiled puppets. A plumpish bathing-suited couple pitched and rolled; one man without a shirt waltzed dreamily to the jazz, his contented face nestled cowlike in his partner's hair; barefooted, three couples spun crazily.

A dog scurried across the floor and scooted under a table. Laughing, Gene looked at Faye, wanting to see her laugh, too. But her face was cemented and set, fascinated by the sound of the musical orgasm, animal-like in its force.

"Gene," she said, "let's dance. Please."

She was up from the chair before Gene could answer.

"I can't dance to that stuff," he groaned.

But she was hurrying through the tables to the floor. She turned to him waiting and impatient, until he came to her.

Gene pulled her close and tried to fast-step around the floor, his gangling shuffles awkwardly jerky to the machine-gun beats of the quintet. Breaking away, she threw herself out from his closeness, a mixture of intensity and relief on her face. Her body rolled and twisted and jerked, responding to the suggestive music.

But she overdid it; she threw herself out in wild
flings; her jerks and rolls and twists became almost
melodramatic; and only when she tried did she slack-
en her wild pace. Then she seemed to realize that her
dancing was overdone, and she gazed at Gene with a
wan, faint shrug in her expression, as if she realized
her dancing was outdated and that she was washed
up.

The quintet stopped. Faye swayed against Gene as
they went toward the edge of the floor; then, quickly,
she straightened and led him to their table.

Moodily she sat down and tried to respond to
Gene's attempts to lift her into light talk with opening questions.

"How are thinks at work?" he asked.

"The same."

She avoided his eyes, fiddling with a button on her
dress, a dress she had just bought in her excitement
of new aliveness, in contrast to her usual plain suits.
Repeatedly now, she toyed with the foam on the top
of her beer, letting her fingertip make circular motions through the fluff-knitted bubbles.

The band came back, and, like an electrical storm,
burst into a fast number. Gene saw interest flush
Faye's face; but her response was now flabby com-
pared to her intoxication when they had first come
into the building.

Playfully he elbowed her in the ribs, physically and
psychologically. "Come on, gal, snap out of it. Up and
at 'em." He cracked his voice, trying to stick a needle
into her moodiness before it ballooned big, before it
puffed into his mind and mood, too, into his sunny-
day happiness.

She ignored his rib-punch, as if she was not conscious he touched her. "Oh, Gene," she murmured,
"it's coming back," her voice scraping her, and him
low and sinking. "The damn sex problem I've got is
coming back and it's been gone for almost a week. I
can't stand it any longer." It had been nearly a week
since she had taken her clothes off in front of Mickey
on the beach.

Suddenly Gene bent toward her, and he heard himself say, "For Christ's sake, Faye, go to bed with me.
Maybe that will help."

"No. That would make me worry even more. I'd feel
even more guilty. It's like fighting a shadow," she
murmured, soft for only him to hear. "Like trying to
hit back at something you can't even see." Despairingly she scraped at the table top.

The band was playing a low, slow number now, the
clarinet slide-gliding along the shoreline of the piece,
along the edge of deep-water music, moaning jazz
with the pull and strength and solidity of the ocean,
slow and placid, with just a ripple where the water
hits a reef, where the clarinet pricks itself on a high
night.

"Dance?" Gene said. His voice was quiet and strong;
it wanted to prop her up.

She nodded no, as Gene expected; for ever since the
night weeks ago when she had danced him repeatedly close to the woman vocalist, she had refused to
dance slow numbers. It was always too hot, or the
floor was too crowded, or she was too tired. Yet, she
never hesitated to dance to fast pieces, flinging herself out wildly, if not with today's abandon, at lease
with the same intensity.

"Come on," he said, and half rose from the chair.

"I don't feel like it, Gene."

Gene started to sit down, but he felt Faye's eyes catch him. He hesitated. Twisting her head, she glanced at the body-locked couples, as if they were making love on the dance floor.

"Okay," she said, taut. "Let's go." Her voice was husky.

Following her, he had barely reached the edge of the floor when she pulled him in to her, sinking herself in to him, pressing herself to him and the crawling music, soft yet hard in his arms, warm and pushing. Against his neck her pressing lips kissed him; the pain-shock was the same as if her lips were teeth. He returned her kiss. She shivered and drew away, involuntarily, then came in to him again, honeyed and warm.

"Gene," she murmured.

Then, quickly, she broke from him and held him away, arm-length, her lips pinched, her head shaking, slowly and perplexed, as if their closeness had been ridiculous and wrong and strange. Murmuring "I'm sorry, Gene," she spun and went to their table.

"What happened?" Gene asked when they sat down, his voice barely audible.

She shrugged and flicked the end of her fingernail against her beer glass; it clanked hollowly, empty. Empty, like the afternoon had become, sievelike, their earlier gaiety gone, drained out through the ducts of Faye's mood.

"I felt like going to bed with you just now," she said. "It made me feel more guilty, like I told you it would."

As the day sank into the evening end of the afternoon, Faye began to drink her beer in fast, nervous gulps, talkless except for an answered, "Not yet," to Gene's suggestion that they leave. Once, when a man gave her a leer-wink as she was returning from the ladies' room, she muttered, "Smart guy," as she sat next to Gene. "Men, think they're all smart guys. How come you aren't a smart guy, Gene?"

Gene ignored her question. He knew she was in a foul mood. Anything he said would simply make matters worse.

At Gene's insistence, they finally left the jazz joint and went out and found a small restaurant and ate sandwiches and drank coffee. Later, in the car, Faye said quietly, "I don't want to go home. Let's stay here all night."

All night. The words swarmed through Gene. All night. Just the two of them.

She spun her head at him, quick, a new vibrancy about her, a fresh enthusiasm in her voice that brought back to Gene the alive Faye on their ride to the lake this afternoon.

"Come on, Gene, let's!" her words snapping and kicking a warm hole in his belly. "We'll get a bottle and some ice and soda. Have a party. Just us."

They got an ancient room, with pictures of grandfather and grandmother hanging on the walls. And with two beds; she had insisted on two.

The fiber rocking chair between the beds groaned as Faye sat down. "My God, Gene, do we have a suite, or do we have a suite." She kicked at a gob of dust under the bed. "All the comforts of home." Squeak! squawk! went the chair. "Music, too," she chuckled.

Then she glanced at the wall, and as Gene followed
her gaze he saw that she was looking at the picture
of grandmother.

Grandmother had on a dreary-black dress, buttoned down the front and choke-tight around her
neck. She had a narrow face, sternly pinched, disap-
proving. Puritanically hard and piercing, she stared
at the unmarried couple in the wedlock room, in
shocked and scandalized accusation, as if she were
saying, "Disgraceful! It's disgraceful!"

Gene snickered. "She doesn't look like the happiest
woman in the world."

"Put something over that picture," Faye said, quietly
strong. Her face was set; there was no smile behind
her words.

Gene shrugged and tucked his handkerchief over
the upper two corners of the picture, letting the cloth
cover Grandmother's face. "Okay?" he asked as he
faced the wall.

He did not see Faye's nod, her expression of anxiety
and uneasiness. Grinning, he turned and started toward her. "Is that okay?"

"Yes." There was a snap in her voice.

Gene stopped at the sight of Faye's forehead-wrin-
kle, deep-cut and shadowy under the single ceiling
light. To change the subject, he asked her if she was
ready for a drink.

"I don't want any," she murmured. "I'm tired, I'm go-
ing to bed." She kicked off one loafer. "You go ahead,
I'm going to bed." Thump! the other shoe hit the floor.
"Turn around," she said.

No gaiety in her voice now, no zip in her movements, no spurt, no fire.

Gene shrugged and turned to the stand and mixed himself a drink. He heard the rustle of Faye's clothing as she undressed, the squeak of the bedsprings.

"All right," she said.

Gene walked to the bed and sat down. She had the covers pulled up around her neck; a bra strap peeped out at him from beneath the top of a sheet. Her slacks were hung on the back of the chair.

"Take a sip," he said, offering her the glass.

"Huh uh."

"Huh uh." Her eyes were closing.

"Hey, don't go to sleep on me."

"I'm beat," she said, yawning. "All of a sudden. Must be the bed."

"Or Grandmother on the wall."

"What do you mean?" she said quickly.

"Grandmother was giving you a helluva look and you couldn't take it."

She glanced at the covered picture. "Yeah, I guess you're right. The old gal makes me feel like an all-night girl."

Gene snorted. "Whoever heard of an all-night girl sleeping by herself?"

Faye grinned, slight and rapid. Then she turned over on her side, her back to Gene, the thin sheet right around her shoulder. "Let's go to sleep," she said.

His hand fluttered across her hair. She did not move. He caressed her arm, gently, tenderly, and looked longingly at the space between her and the edge of the bed. He flicked off the light, undressed as far as his shorts and undershirt, and lay down beside her, his arm thrown carelessly over her waist. Thump! she butted him with her rear. He took his arm from around her, quickly. She bumped him again. "Get in your own bed," she said.

"I like it better here." He put his arm around her again.

This time she turned to him, moaning a little, a mixture of passion and depression. She tenderly snuggled her head in under his chin. "Oh, Gene, I want you so much. But I'm afraid to do anything, like I told you before."

"But don't you see, if we made love and it satisfied you, then you wouldn't want Mickey."

With that, he ignored her "No, Gene, please," and unbuttoned her bra strap and took one of her large, full breasts to his lips and kissed until she was pushing against him and moaning. He felt her hot, seeking hand go down his body.

CHAPTER NINE

Gene hadn't been in the *Press* the following Monday morning more than a few minutes when Mickey came up, her grin almost a smirk. She approached him in a corner of the newsroom where they could have privacy.

"Heard you and Faye did a little weekending together," she chuckled.

"Yeah?" Gene said, noncommittal.

"Uh huh. Understand you two really slept around."

"You hear a lot of things these days."

Mickey nodded. "Especially from girls who get back from weekends and do some phoning. They're so tired, you know, that they can't come around. They have to phone."

"Faye phoned you?" Gene asked, alarmed.

"Of course. Last night. She always does. Just had to tell me about what a lover-boy you turned out to be." She grinned sarcastically. "Who would have thought it of our tender, sensitive young man." She snickered. "Man, did she sound tired. What *did* you do to our innocent young girl? And did you *have* to do it all weekend? My Gawd, doll, Faye may be a bed-honey kid, but after all she's not a pro like me."

"I don't believe you" was all Gene could manage.

"I got it on tape, honey. It says plain."

Anger suddenly surged in Gene. "Why don't you mind your own business?" he snapped.

Ruffled, Mickey snapped back, but keeping her voice low. "Why don't you mind yours! I was taking care of Faye until you came along."

"You! What do you mean, *you* were taking care of her. Who in the hell are you!"

"Me? I'm the gal who won't get her pregnant, that's who."

"Nobody's getting her pregnant."

"Stay away from her, then."

"That's my business!"

"It's mine, too, doll!"

Mickey's voice had become loud, and Mark heard her last words. He stepped quietly in between them, and took Gene back to his desk.

"Easy," Mark said. "Easy."

"Bitch," Gene muttered. "Who in the hell does she think she is?"

"You take care of Faye. I'll handle Mickey."

"Why in the hell did Faye want to phone *her*?"

"They've known each other for years."

"It's no good, Mark. You know it as well as I do."

"Don't worry about it. I'll take care of Mickey. You go after Faye."

Gene was sitting at his desk, and he got up slowly, putting his hand on Mark's arm, feeling its strength, at ease suddenly. He wanted to hug the man.

"You're a good guy, you know it," Gene said. "I like you a helluva lot."

When Mark went back to his desk Gene still felt the strength of his arm, a strength he carried with him when he phoned Faye later in the day and asked her, casually, why she had phoned Mickey.

"Oh, I just felt like it," she said, the surprise of Gene's knowing of the call in her voice. "How did you find out?"

"Mickey told me."

"Oh."

"She'll spread it all around, Faye."

"No she won't. She won't tell it to anyone but you."

"Why just me?"

She hesitated. "She's jealous of you."

Just before quitting time Faye phoned him from work. She was nervous and disturbed, and she asked him to pick her up in front of her office building; she couldn't wait until eight; would he please hurry?

She was waiting for him when he drove up, her expression tense and masklike. Before he could lean over and swing open the door she was in the car, sliding over close to him, gripping his leg as he drove to his apartment. As soon as they were inside the apartment, a small furnished one-bedroom place, she was clinging to him, pushing her head into his shoulder and neck, her body straining at him. He mixed her a drink and they sat on the sofa and she relaxed, but her fingers still dug into his leg, much like, Gene thought, his hand had tightened around Mark's arm.

"It was Mickey," she said. "She came into the office this afternoon. I was sitting at my desk working and I looked up and there she was staring at me with that funny kind of grin of hers. Just staring at me, right in front of everybody. Just staring at me until I felt like jumping up and running. I've never had one person scare me so much."

The words jumped out of Faye, thin and breaking, sprung out like bundles of knotted tension.

"She never said a word the whole time she was there. I asked her what she wanted and why she was there and all that, but she never said a word. And all those people there looking. I felt like a fool. And she wouldn't leave, and she wouldn't say anything. I felt like sinking into the floor, or screaming, or something. It was awful. That grin of hers, that horrible grin. I never want to see her again. Never

"Finally I got up and went to the ladies' room. Didn't know where I was going when I started. When I came back she was gone. That's when I phoned you. And the people at work, what do they think? Nobody said a word to me the rest of the day, except when it was necessary. That grin of hers, oh God.

"Oh, Gene, let's get away from here. Let's go away someplace together."

They went away together the next Saturday, the Saturday before Labor Day. They told Faye's parents the same story they had used the weekend before, that they were accompanied by a married couple. By nightfall, as they were coming into Chicago, they passed a nightclub with neon dancing girls flashing over the entrance. Impulsively, Gene suggested that they see a striptease.

Faye giggled nervously. "I don't know. I've never seen one before."

"We won't stay long. Come on. Just for kicks."

"If you want to."

They drove into a parking lot adjoining the club, then walked in under a canopied entrance and went into the gymlike structure. At once Gene heard Faye's sharp intake of breath, low and barely audible. "My God," she murmured.

She did not seem to notice the headwaiter, a tall smilingly polite man. "Two, sir?" he asked.

Gene nodded and, puzzled at the intensity of Faye's stare on a wiggling stripteaser, he followed the waiter through the half-filled club to a table close to the dance floor.

"My God," Faye repeated as they sat down, her voice both fascinated and shocked.

A big-bosomed waitress asked for their order. Gene ordered a beer. But Faye did not seem to realize the waitress was there; she was conscious only of the snakelike movements, the sensual bumps and grinds of the stripteaser.

"Faye, what do you want?"

She did not answer. Her face was flushed into a sort of horrible fascination as she stared at the pulsating sensuality of the stripper. She seemed to strain toward the dancer, to feel with her the intoxicating wail of the crawling music, the thump of the drum at each hip-rolling, pushing movement of the painted woman.

"Faye!" Gene blurted.

The waitress shifted impatiently and glared at Faye with a disgusted weariness.

"Bring us two beers," Gene snapped. "Anything."

He felt a sudden strange sinking at the look on Faye's face; a numb knot crawled heavily into his stomach.

He looked quickly at the stripper. She was down to her G-string and a transparent net across her breasts. Her hands flitted up and down her waist, caressing herself. Infatuated, Faye watched the woman toy with her nipples, circling her finger around and around the brown-pointed tips, teasingly coy, with a smirking smile on her pancaked-pretty face.

With a jolt, Gene remembered the image of Faye's forefinger going around and around through beer foam in the same manner in which the dancer now worked her finger around the brown of her breast.

He reached for Faye's arm and felt the hard-knotted muscles. She did not turn her head. She would not look at him.

The club was thick with cigarette smoke. Dim lights spotted the room, white faces showing in the background. A colored spotlight was on the dancer. Seductive music skidded across the floor and up the woman's near-naked body. A musical orgasm. Faye's face was granitely set. The stripper kept squatting on the floor, her knees bent, her thighs raising her up and down, up down, slow, slow, her split legs going up and down up and down, as she smiled crookedly. Her finger teasingly danced up her leg and thigh as the music sank into her and the crowd, and into excited Faye.

Then Faye was gone. She had sprung up from her seat, had squirmed in between the tables, her back to the stripper.

Gene saw her walk rapidly into the restroom.

The woman flicked off her breast net, bounced her heavy-hung boobies at the audience, rubbed them in the face of the baldheaded ringsider, and with a departing bounce of her naked rump, retired from the floor.

The show was intermissioned, the lights came up.

Gene's gaze rested on the door to the ladies' room. He felt numb at the sudden and peculiar disappearance of Faye, the way she jumped up almost as if she could not sit there any longer and watch the dancer, as if she were escaping. A frown creased and cracked the bubbles of sweat which stuck to his forehead.

In the intermission lights he glanced around the interior of the club, at the checkerboard tablecloths, the paste-white faces of patrons, most of whom were disinterested. They were like stone statues with occasional lip movements. Atmosphered in the period of the gay nineties, the walls of the club were covered with murals which depicted the decade. The horse-drawn streetcar, the front of a bar with nickel beers advertised, the bicycle built for two, the girl with the strawberry curls who flirted with the boy with striped suit and straw hat. Behind the bar, which ran against the wall on Gene's right, was the picture of the gay philosopher, beer suds, whiskers, crinkly grin and all. The bartender had a walrus mustache, the waitresses wore pink stockings, the place had a personality.

Faye came back from the ladies' room and sat down.

"Had to go in a hurry," she murmured.

There was nervousness in her voice, a slight tremble in her hand as she picked up her glass of beer.

"So I noticed," he grinned. "You must have been great at the hundred-yard dash in high school."

She tried to smile. Her lips lifted and arched; but quickly, as if heavy and burdensome, they sagged.

Gene prodded her with small talk, trying to knife through the mattress of her sudden disinterest. Faye grunted her answers, laughing mechanically at his sly-funny remarks, as if she wanted to come over with him and have a good time, as if she didn't want to ruin their evening and their weekend. Yet there was an effort in her attempts at casualness. She worked at being a good sport.

The orchestra came back and slid into a slow-beating foxtrot.

"Dance?" Gene said.

He saw her hesitancy, but then her expression lightened.

"Okay," she said.

She came in close to him on the dance floor, resting her body against his, yet with a coolness, with a detachment. Within his arms, her presence danced away from him.

When the number was over, she turned, not harshly, not with anger or impatience, and quietly walked off the floor.

"You having a good time?" she said when they sat down.

"If you are."

She shrugged. "I don't know if I am or not."

"Let's go," he said.

She hesitated: her forehead wrinkle creased deep. "Not yet," she said.

"What's eating you?" His voice was cottonishly soft.

"Nothing."

"Something happened when we came in here. I mean, more than just seeing a stripper for the first time."

She nodded; her eyes were distant.

"Just the stripper?"

"Maybe," she said. "I don't know."

"We better go, then. They'll bring on another one in a few minutes."

He could see her rubbing the palm of her hand across the table in nervous digs at the cloth.

"Hell, I really don't believe you've never seen a teaser before." His words were light with incredulity. He couldn't imagine sophisticated Faye being sheltered from burlesque. Surely she had cat-called at the phoniness of the stripteaser, had flipped pennies to the sex-wigglers. "When you said you hadn't outside I thought you were kidding."

She shook her head. "Never wanted to."

"You haven't missed much."

"I don't know. This girl seemed to be on the ball."

"She's better than average," Gene admitted.

"She can really throw herself around, all right," Faye said. "But nobody seems to be watching her."

"Aah, this stuff gets old as hell after a while." He raised an eyebrow at her. "But don't tell me *you* saw who was looking at her and who wasn't." He grinned wryly. "You just had eyes for the wiggler."

"Well, after all," she said stiffly, "this is the first time I've ever seen a woman take her clothes off in public."

Gene chuckled. "I believe that all right. You stared at her like you were hypnotized."

"I wasn't staring at her! I know what a naked woman looks like. I'm not a man."

Gene didn't say anything. Was she a man or was she a woman? he thought.

"I think she did a good job of taking them off, too. There's something about it, that..." She paused, groping for a word. "That seems beautiful."

"Beautiful!" Gene snorted. He laughed.

Faye bristled. "All you think about is the sex in it. Just like a man," she muttered.

The orchestra had stopped playing while Gene and Faye were talking. After a cigarette-smoking break the musicians came back to the bandstand. A flourish of drums, a spotlighted circle on the dance floor, and a man with a thin-bent nose, top-hatted and lean, stepped up to a microphone.

His face was expressionless, sallowly bored, the color of old dough. The roll of drums flattened out, stopped; the audience quieted, the MC spoke:

"And now ladies and gentlemen we give you our lovely and exotic dancing girls."

The words rolled out of him with continuous regularity, monotonous and dead. He stepped off the dance floor, dragging the microphone behind him.

The strippers came on. Big-bosomed or flat-chested, bony-legged or sausagelike, stringbeaned or limaed, the girls bumped and ground onto the floor, one following the other in the declothing process.

One girl was particularly pitiful to Gene. She was young, middle-teened, little-boned and limply frightened. Trembling, she began to revolve her hips in a hopelessly amateurish attempt at stripping; her skinny body jerked and jumped far outside the drum beat, a twitching, loose-jointed puppet, lonely and cryingly sad.

One or two hard, humorless laughs broke from the audience.

The girl began to tug at the zipper in her strip-dress. As the crowd howled, she fumbled for the metal clasp. Her face crimsoned, and with a desperate snatch at the zipper she let the flimsy garment fall around her ankles. Frantically now, she stripped her series of bras and step-outs, down to her loose-fitting G-string.

Her body was rib-studded, her breasts flabby. When she ran off the floor, her skinny buttocks looked incongruously white and tiny against the black wall of howling spectators.

The crowd was roaring, the crowd was stuffed with glee.

Gene swiveled his head at Faye. "Let's get the hell out of here!" he snapped.

But the MC had dragged the microphone back into the spotlight. He held up his hand for silence.

"And now ladies and gentlemen we are proud to present the lovely and fabulous star of our show, Shim, in her exotic and sensual Dance-of-the-Two-Selves."

A murmur in the crowd, an anticipation.

"What's this Dance-of-the-Two-Selves thing?" Faye said.

Gene shrugged. "You got me."

The MC pulled the microphone off the floor and the spotlight went out. Complete blackness. Cigarettes red-dotted the club. Coughs, and the silence of waiting.

Then steps on the dance floor, the rustle of clothing.

The spotlight flashed on. Shim stood in the center of the floor.

She was dressed half as a man and half as a woman. A cap flopped on one side of her head; on the other

side her hair was fluffed and curled. She wore a tux-
edo on half of her body, complete with black oxfords;
on the other half, a sex-tight dress. Her lipstick was
divided in the center. One eyebrow was thin-plucked
and darkened. She wore a man's ring on her right
hand, her fingernails painted on the other.

"My God!" Faye blurted.

Gene grinned. But, noticing the rigidity of Faye's
face, her look of horror and fright, together with an
eerie fascination, his grin soured and slid away.

The music began to throb, deep-pitched and moaning. Shim had her man's half to the audience, the cap
pulled low to the side of her head and partially cov-
ering her face. Slowly, she took her hand out of her
pocket and slid it across the front of her body to her
other arm, the woman-arm.

"Gene," Faye mumbled.

Shim held the "woman" by the wrist, pulling "her"
to "him," then flicking "his" fingers up to "her" shoulder, sensually, in rough-fast caresses.

The music quickened.

Spinning around, Shim had the "woman" next to
the audience; the man-hand skipped up and down
her side, her back, her thigh, down her leg. The fingers picked at a zipper in the dress, then jumped to
her breast. Gradually the "man" began to bend Shim
back.

"Gene," Faye whimpered. She gripped his arm. Her
expression was anguished yet miserably fascinated.
Her chest jumped with quick breathing. "I can't stand
this," she moaned.

"Let's go." Gene started to get up.

"No, wait!" she said quickly. She pulled him back into the chair. "I'm all right. This will be over in a minute."

Shim sank back, the "man" over her, forcing her down. "His" hand skipped from her breast, down her leg to yank her dress up over her hip.

Faye moved. She strained forward over the table.

Shim pushed the "man" back up and straightened herself higher and shoved "his" arm and hand away from her body.

The music was beating in a fast throb; the audience staringly silent.

Shim struggled with herself. The man half bent the woman half back, his hand ripped under her dress, then tore the clothing from her breasts. Shim screamed; she fought up from the floor; she screamed again and ran.

The "man" caught her at ringside and forced her back, back.

Shim's hair was touching the floor, the music was a wild yell. In the rear of the club, patrons stood on their chairs.

Although Faye could easily see the bending Shim, she jumped up, still holding Gene's arm, vise-like.

Back, back, slowly, the "man" forced Shim down to the floor, down; her head touched the wood, her shoulders flattening, down. She moaned, she sagged, she collapsed.

Her dress twisted around her waist, Shim lay on her back, the "man" folded over her, "his" hand yanking at her, yanking at her.

The spotlight went out.

Faye was trembling as she sat down, and Gene felt her grip on his wrist weaken. He put his arm around her waist. Her summer dress was damp; it stuck to her skin.

"Let's get out of this place," she mumbled.

She got up and started walking through the stove-black club toward the exit. She hit a chair but she didn't stop moving. Gene grabbed for her and missed.

"Wait 'til the lights go on," he said.

She didn't answer. Stumbling against chairs and tables, bumping into other patrons, almost frantically she fought toward the door.

As Gene went after her, the lights came on. He caught her at the club entrance.

"Wait a minute, I got to get the check," he said.

"I'll be in the car." She broke away from him and went out.

CHAPTER TEN

Gene left the nightclub and started through Chicago with Faye, rigidly silent, slumped in the corner of the front seat, staring out at the starting rain, which came in slow patters at first, then harder, until wind-driven water was slamming against the car.

"We won't be able to go far in this stuff," Gene said.

He glanced at Faye. Her head to the side, shifting with motions of the car, she had fallen into her forgetting sleep. He crept along a street forlornly machine-gunned by rain, peering ahead until he saw a motel. He stopped, woke Faye up, and was about to dash inside when she stopped him with a serious and quiet, "Just get one room, Gene."

"I am," he said.

"I don't want to be by myself tonight. I want you with me. All night."

He slid across the seat and held her close.

"I feel lousy," she said. "I don't want to see any more stripteasers. They make me feel dirty."

"Forget it."

"I can't. That woman, that half-and-half thing." She spun her head in disgusted and frightened jerks, as if she were trying to shake Shim from her memory, yet, too, was afraid that she couldn't. "Let's go in," she said.

A weary clerk gave them a room. It was smallish, yet modern and clean, with a double bed and a bath.

"Not bad," Gene said.

Faye nodded and flopped across the bed.

"I'm so tired," she murmured.

Gene sat down beside her and let his hand rest on one leg, playfully slapping the calf.

"Looks like we won't get on the beach until tomorrow.

His voice scratched him, and he laughed, quick and hollow, smoothing the nervous pricks out of it. He slapped the leg again; his hand inched down to her ankle.

"We'll get up bright and early tomorrow, huh?"

His eyes were resting on her body, her full hips, the slender waist where it dipped with the dip of the bed, her disheveled hair, a liquid black overflow onto the pillow she had pulled under her head.

She yawned and stretched and Gene watched her body go hard and taut across the bed.

He began to knead the small of her back.

She purred. "Ummmm, that feels good." She relaxed and folded into the bed like an old purring cat. "You're a better back-rubber than my mother."

"Uh huh."

He swallowed the dryness out of his throat and sank slowly down beside her, one elbow propped under him. Slowly, he pushed and squeezed at her back and shoulders.

"Hmmmmm," she intoned.

"I guess you know I charge for this service."

"Bill me."

He pulled her toward him, tenderly, his face in her hair, clean smelling now with no perfume. Just to have her nestle in next to him, be quiet and warm with him, together, lying apart, yet together. At least for a while; afterwards, action!

"Faye," he murmured, with the weight of her warmth in his voice, the burr scratch of her name buried deep in her hair.

She moved, and he felt her stiffen and draw away from him.

Drawing away from him. His hand slipped from her side, then fell from her back. She was drawing away from him and he let her go.

"We better go to bed," she said. She sat up and yawned. Her face was pink-wrinkled from the bed-spread.

"Guess so."

Faye went in the bath and got into her pajamas. Then Gene. When he came back into the room, she was snuggled under the covers, her back to the center of the bed.

"Ready for lights out?"

"Uh huh."

He snapped the wall switch and climbed in beside her.

He lay on his back, away from her. Carefully he lowered his hands to his side, keeping them pinned to his hips, flattening out his breathing. He didn't want to get excited and then be pushed away again. Outside, a car swished by, splattering the sound of rain on the street, a loud sound in the quiet of the room. He listened. Faye's breathing was quick and climbing. He felt the heat of her body, and he ached to slide over and press close and hold her.

Then she was turning to him.

Gene stiffened, feeling something bang against the inside of his chest. She was on her side now, still moving toward him. He saw her hands come out of the covers, saw her rise a little on her elbow.

Then her arms were around him. Her fingers pressed into his back; her body forced in close and pushing. He felt her lips come, soft yet hard, against his. Her hand skipped up and down his back, stopping at inch-intervals to pull him in closer to her.

She was high up on one elbow now, half over him, her moist lips on his neck, thrusting her body at him, almost desperately, almost frantically.

"Gene. Gene."

His fingers fumbled with her pajama top. Trying to help him, she ripped it off in her frenzy. Then she kicked off the bottoms. Before Gene could take of his own pajamas, she took them off for him...and then took him.

Later, she began to cry, quietly, sobbing. He tenderly caressed her.

"Did you like that?" she asked after a moment.

"Yes."

"I can do that for you, but that's all I can do." She turned her face to the wall.

"I'm a virgin," she said. "I've told you before." Her voice was empty. "I'm going to stay that way until I get married."

A train whistled in the distance, then died.

"*If* I get married," she mumbled.

CHAPTER ELEVEN

They had a leisurely breakfast close to the motel the next morning, then drove fifty-odd miles to the lake resort. They finally found a vacancy in a second-rate hotel on Back Alley Avenue. Their room was almost closet-small. With sweat bubbling on her forehead, a smiling resignation in her eyes, Faye looked at the eave-formed ceiling and the old iron bed.

"We should have made a reservation," Gene managed to say.

"An excellent observation."

"It's cheap, anyway," he said weakly.

"It should be."

A hot day, they got into their suits immediately and walked the half dozen blocks to the lake. Faye's full, soft body looked like a piece of strolling heaven in a bathing suit. The beach was packed with a writing mass of near-nakedness. Gene took off his tee shirt. "Come on, let's go in," he said.

They dived into the lake together and came up spitting watery laughs. Faye began to swim out, away from Gene and the shoreline, taking sweeping, strong strokes. Gene plunged in after her, and as she turned parallel to the beach, he caught her. They swam slowly together until Faye suddenly turned and slivered toward the shore.

"Race you in!" she yelled.

Gene went after her.

She was rested and waiting for him when he struggled out of the lake.

"Slowpoke," she laughingly spat.

"Too many cigarettes," Gene mumbled. "Too much beer."

He took her by the waist, and they walked toward their spot on the beach. He felt her steady, quiet gaze on his face as they sat down at the spot.

"Gene, everything's still the same with us, isn't it?" Her voice was hesitant and unsure.

"Sure." He looked at her curiously.

"I mean...last night in bed. And last week, too."

He grinned.

"I don't know what happened. All of a sudden I just went haywire. Just felt like...well, like having you, I guess."

"Happens all the time."

"And that was true, what I said about being a virgin."

She was pawing the sand with her toes, her downcast face embarrassed.

"I guess you don't believe me," she said.

Gene hesitated; then, cautiously keeping his voice light, he said, "Well, frankly, it's a little hard to believe, as much as you used to get around."

She looked up at him, a wan smile under the seriousness of her expression.

"I'll show you some day. Maybe."

"Maybe you won't, too."

She laughed, a cover-up, let's-change-the-subject laugh, unfunny, coughlike and forced.

"Let's forget it and go drink some beer," she said.

Gene frowned. "I want to eat, not drink."

"You can eat, I'm not hungry. Come on."

Faye led the way into the first bar-restaurant she saw, a beachfront spot, sandy-floored, crowded with bathing-suited swimmers who lounged at the tables and booths. A jukebox blared in a corner.

Gene ordered a sandwich and iced tea; Faye, a bottle of beer.

"Don't you ever get tired of drinking that stuff?" Gene said through a mouthful of ham, mayonnaise, and tomato.

"Huh uh. Beer's good for you, makes you fat. See what it's done for me." She grinned and ordered another bottle. "Let me buy you one. No use you paying for everything while we're here."

Faye kept drinking steadily, more than Gene had ever seen her consume, once going up to the bar and getting a beer herself when she couldn't get the waitress's attention. Gene shook off her offers. "Full," he said. Soon though, Faye's chatter stopped and she became moodily silent.

"Let's go for a swim," he suggested, hoping to stick a pin in her ballooning depression.

"Huh uh. I feel like drinking."

"You can't drink all afternoon. You'll be logy by tonight."

She shrugged. "I can take care of myself. You go on in if you want to."

Faye drank all afternoon. She either ignored Gene's urging to go back to their room or she told him to "go on if you want to, I'm not stopping you," growing more depressed and irritable as the day ground on. She began her forefinger-in-beer routine, her eyes glazed and blank as she stared out the open front of the restaurant at the evening boardwalk strollers.

"Look at 'em," she said. Her voice bitterly hard. "On parade. Think they're pretty."

"Forget it, will ya."

"Think they're hot stuff. Bunch of aristocrats walking around looking at the common herd. Hi, Duchess," she said to an elderly woman, who, after looking curiously at Faye, continued on up the beachfront.

"Faye, keep quiet." He heard a snicker behind him.

"Don't tell me to keep quiet."

Gene stood up. "Come on, let's get out of here."

Faye did not move. "I'm comfortable where I am." Her eyes were glassily sharp. "And I'm still thirsty. Hey, waitress. One more."

The waitress scowled and brought Faye a beer. Gene paid her and turned to Faye.

Holding his voice steady, he said, "Look, I'm going back to the room and get dressed. If you want to come with me, okay. If you don't, that's okay, too."

"That's nice of you," she said.

"You're drunk."

"Good!"

He got up. "Are you coming, or aren't you?"

"Are you propositioning me, sir?" She smiled at the titter which broke from the surrounding tables.

Gene blurted a profanity and strode out onto the boardwalk. Faye followed him, an alcoholic-flushed smirk on her face. Gene took her arm and tried to lead her down the boardwalk. She jerked away from him.

"Keep your hands off me."

Evening-clean strollers stared in disgust at the un-steady woman, the young man prodding her along, embarrassed. Faye deliberately returned their stares. A sarcastic smile slit her face. She nodded elaborately polite, "Hello," at the upturned nose of an old-maid-ish woman, who snorted and waddled away leading her Yorkshire terrier.

Fay snickered, "Well, what do you know!" as they approached a lakefront hotel. A group of men and women, paunched and rusty-aged, resting in rockers, were on the hotel's jutting front porch.

"Look at all the old folks at home!" she greeted as she stopped in front of them.

One woman looked curiously at Faye and stopped fanning.

"Shut up!" Gene hissed.

"Hi, old crows!" Faye snorted.

She resisted Gene's attempts to push her past the hotel.

"For Christ's sake, Faye, let's go."

She walked up to the edge of the porch and stopped in front of a solid-meated woman.

"What are you doing? Waiting for the navy to come in?"

The woman avoided her stare. A man coughed slightly and colored.

"Does the passing parade suit you!" she screeched. She turned to Gene. "Look at 'em! My God! look what old age dragged in!"

Gene jabbed her in the ribs. "Come on! come on!"

"Old phonies!"

Grabbing her arm, Gene pulled her away from the hotel.

She began to laugh, not loud, but low and bitter and humorless as she weaved up the boardwalk at Gene's side.

"Did you see 'em?" she said. "The old phonies. I shocked 'em, all right. Sitting out there, bunch of old hens, sitting out there on the porch with their husbands. So respectable." She lurched and laughed. "I shocked 'em, showed 'em what I thought of them."

"Yeah, yeah." Placating her now, easing off the boardwalk up the street toward the hotel.

As they crossed an intersection, an ancient she-dog, wrinkle-teated with twelve swaying sags, waddled in front of a car. Brakes screeched; the car stopped. Unhurried, the dog continued on to the opposite curb.

Faye howled. "Look at the old woman!" she shrieked. "Motherhood. The power of motherhood. Here, mother." Weaving, she bent down in the middle of the street and snapped her fingers at the dog. "Here, mother mother mother mother."

The dog ignored her and swayed into a can-filled alley.

With gentle force, Gene prodded Faye to the curb.

"Nothing like being a mother," she said. "Nothing like turning out kids like a machine. Really keeps the body in trim. Got a cigarette?"

Gene held a flame to her wavering cigarette.

"I can hardly wait to have about sixty-two screaming kids. Must be wonderful to see your belly get big with brats. I can hardly wait. Hot to go for those babies. Hot. That's me, Gene. Hot. Just like Mickey says. I'll have to go to that place with her that she's always trying to get me to go to. The Intimate. Sounds hot, doesn't it. That's for me. If it's for me."

Gene watched her deliberately walk in front of a group of pedestrians, forcing them to dodge her. In their hotel lobby, she stared insolently at an elderly woman in front of the desk. Ridiculously grinning, she gave the woman an elaborate bow.

She bowed too far. She stumbled, slipped on a small rug, and was falling when Gene caught her and led her to the elevator.

As soon as she got in their room, she took off her bathing suit and stood naked in front of Gene. "Look at me," she mumbled. "Look at me. I'm a woman, see. I got all the equipment." She cupped her full breasts. "Feel." She came to Gene and he felt their round softness. "See, I got everything a man wants. I'm a woman." She sat on the bed. "When a man looks at me, he knows I'm a woman." She snorted, disgusted and drunkenly. "But damn it! I don't feel like a woman— at least, a lot of times. I'm sort of half and half, like that damn stripper we saw, that Shim. I'm like her, like a damn mixed-up stripteaser!"

Then she lay back naked on the bed and began to cry. Gene lay beside her until she went to sleep. He pulled a sheet over her. He knew why she had got drunk and acted the way she did this afternoon. She had done it because she hated herself the way she was. She had done it because she was trying to forget herself in drink, the self that she hated.

"Gene."

Somebody was shaking him by the shoulder.

"Gene, wake up."

It was Faye's voice, he finally realized, as her hand tugged at his arm. He blinked and opened his eyes. The light was on. Faye stood beside the bed, dressed.

Her suitcase was on a chair, as if she had just packed it.

"What d'ya want?" He yawned and rubbed his hand across his eyes.

She sat down beside him. Her eyes were cloudy-red and swollen. Even with fresh makeup, her face looked haggard.

"I've got to go home," she said. Her voice cracked.

He was instantly awake, propped up on one elbow. "Go home?"

She nodded. "I've got to."

Gene looked at his wristwatch. Almost four a.m.

"I'm worried about mother and..." She turned her head away from him. "Everything."

"Let's wait until daylight anyway."

She said, "No," weakly.

Outside, he heard a car's horn blow emptily loud in the before-dawn quiet.

"Helluva time to leave," he said.

She sniffled.

"Please take me home," she said.

"Well, if I got to..."

She turned to him. "I'm sorry about what happened yesterday. At that beer place." Her eyes were cryingly wet.

"Forget it."

"You should have stopped me from drinking so much. I'm not used to that much beer." She looked at the floor. "I don't remember...what I did. There were some women on a porch, weren't there?"

Gene nodded reluctantly.

She swallowed. "Oh, God," she moaned. She turned her head away.

Gene reached out and folded her in to him. His hand slid soothingly down and up her back.

"Sh-sh," he murmured.

"I didn't even know those people," she sobbed. "What did I want to talk to them like that for? God, oh, God." She sniffled. "Losing my mind. That's what's happening, I'm losing my mind. Going batty. Screwy."

"Sh-sh."

"I've never done anything like this before...this bad. Crazy, that's me. Dirty. I feel dirty."

Gene swung over the side of the bed and pulled on his pants.

"One thing, won't be much traffic this time of the morning."

He dressed quickly while Faye finished packing her suitcase. A little after four o'clock they were on the highway. Faye sat silently, smoking cigarette after cigarette. They stopped once for coffee; she stared moodily into her cup.

Coming into Chicago, Gene saw her head jerk, her body stiffen and strain forward.

"Look out ahead!" she shouted.

He peered ahead at the pavement. The road was clear.

"You're going to hit that woman!" she screamed. She threw her arms in front of her face.

Mechanically, Gene put on the brakes: but, seeing nothing in the road, he pushed the gas pedal down again.

"What are you talking about? I didn't see any woman."

He heard her sob. Her face was buried in her hands.

Slowing the car, he started to pull off the pavement.

"Don't stop!" she shouted.

"There wasn't any woman, Faye. Nobody in the road."

"Keep going! For God sake's, Gene! keep going!"

He trounced on the gas; the car bucked forward.

"I still didn't see any woman," he murmured.

"She floated away," Faye mumbled. "She floated right into the woods."

Faye cried softly as they went through Chicago.

CHAPTER TWELVE

During the week after the striptease incident, Gene phoned Faye every night. She would answer wearily in a drooping voice.

"See you tonight?" he'd ask.

"I'm sorry, Gene, but I feel lousy tonight."

Or she was too tired.

Or she had studying to do.

She had gone back to her night classes at Chelsor College with a gritty, pushing singleness of mind. "There's only one thing left for me," she said. "Learn as much as I can while I still have time."

"What d'ya mean, 'while I still have time'? You have your whole life."

She had shrugged and said, "Maybe."

But at the end of the week Faye phoned Gene. Would he *please* come get her. She was at home.

"Hurry," she said. "Father's on a drunk."

All the lights in the Sherritt house were on when Gene drove up. As he went up the front walk, he heard feet scrambling up the inside stairs and a shouting male voice. He rang the bell and almost immediately the door was jerked open.

"What do *you* want!"

Mr. Sherritt, drunkenly angry, stood in the door-way. Weaving, he gripped the doorknob, his face and lips twisted into a snarl.

"What do you keep coming here for! Who do you think you are, coming here all the time! Nobody here wants to see you, why don't you go home!"

He leaned toward Gene as Gene stepped back on the porch.

"Faye wants a man, not you! You aren't a man! What do you keep coming around here for! You aren't a man. I know what you are, I know all about you! You're a queer!"

He lunged drunkenly forward as Gene backed to the edge of the porch, laughing a high-pitched squeal that tore his mouth wide. "Has to run. Little boy has to run."

Then, stone-faced, Faye was behind her father; she ducked under his arm and came out the door. "Come on," she urged. She grabbed Gene by the wrist and pulled him down the front walk.

They got in the car. Faye was taut and trembling.

"Quick!" she said. "Let's go!"

Gene roared out from the curb.

"You bitch!" the man screamed. He was running down the sidewalk, and as Faye glanced back, she saw him trip on a piece of loose cement. Stumbling, he fell heavily on the lawn and lay still.

"Stop, Gene." Faye's voice, now frightened, the anger gone.

Gene mashed the brakes; the car skidded to a halt.

Faye sprang out the door. Gene saw her coat fly out behind her as she dashed toward the front yard. Like pistons, her legs churned over the street, the side-walk, and yard, running to help her drunken father.

As Gene dashed after Faye, he saw her bend over her father and try to pull the man up. He pushed her away.

"Get away from me, you bitch!"

Gene stopped.

"I don't want your dirty hands on me!" he father said.

Faye took a step back; her hands dangled at her side. Then she turned and came back to Gene, her face masklike. Together, they walked back to the car.

They drove without direction, Faye sucking on one cigarette after another, flicking the ashes nervously out of the window. Finally she mumbled, "You came to the house too quickly, Gene. I didn't have time to get out front." Then she slid back into her moody quiet.

Gene drove another mile before he could get up enough nerve to say, "Your father called me a queer." He wanted to tell Faye this so that he could hear her deny the accusation. He needed somebody's denial. He wasn't sure if he was a man.

Instead, Faye said, "I like you the way you are, Gene."

"What do you mean by that?"

"I like men who aren't too manly."

"Goddam it, I'm a man." But, actually, he wasn't sure.

"You don't act like one sometimes. The very fact that you go around with me, for example. I'm not very feminine. Most men wouldn't fool around with me,

I'm too masculine for 'em. You know, I go for Mickey, and she's a lesbian."

Gene was silent.

"And you go for her, too. You're attracted to a lesbian. Do you think that's very manly? She told me you two made love down on the beach the other night. Was she any good?" Faye smiled. "I don't blame you for making love to her. I'm certainly not doing you any good—except in that substitute way."

Gene couldn't deny any of the things she had said, so he stayed silent.

"And you're attracted to Mark, too. I can tell—the way you like to be around him so much. Do you think that's very manly?" She chuckled bitterly. "We make a fine pair, we do."

"Maybe we ought to get married," Gene said, half joking, half serious.

But Faye's answer was all the way serious. "I can't marry you, Gene, the way I am. Our life would be horrible. I'd be attracted to lesbians all the time, and you'd worry yourself sick about it. It would be a helluva life for you. The lesbian life is a terrible world. Have you ever seen it?"

"No."

"Well, I'll show you. Drive to the Intimate. That's the place where Mickey hangs out. She's taken me there before. That's where she wanted to take Bo, remember?"

It started to rain, a bursting thunderstorm, with cracks of lightning that somewhere had struck a telephone pole and blackened the countryside. Houses were dark now, dead, like stores and gas stations and restaurants. Like Faye under a street light. Dead. The sky was dead, heavily wet, squatting obscenely on the man and the woman and the speeding car. The dead sky and Faye and the gloating rain.

When they reached the Intimate, Faye led the way through the entrance. Inside, it was dusky with lights kept low and indirect. Gene saw only women. No men. Women in slacks, lipstickless, lounging against the bar, hair slicked back, manlike. One woman sitting at a table of four, her close-cut hair combed straight back, looked quickly and curiously at Gene, then at Faye. Gene felt the sudden tenseness in Faye's arm, her wire-taut rigidity, and heard her heightened breathing as she stared back at the seated woman. For a moment. Then Faye seemed to tear her eyes away, force herself to turn. Woodenly, she moved toward a booth, sitting so that her back was to the woman at the table, her face a moon-white mask.

"Not here, Faye. Please."

"Sit down, Gene," she said dryly.

Women danced close to the jukebox. One giggled and Gene saw the female six-footer who was with her smile and move close and whisper into her ear.

Gene could see the pain and the fear in Faye's face, and the ache in her eyes. He looked away. Strangely frightened, he could not look at her.

"Nice, isn't it," she said. Her voice was bitter and self-hurting.

A waitress with a rumbly voice took their order and returned with two bottles of beer.

Two women were in the booth in front of them, one with her arm around the other. They kissed passionately.

"Let's get out of this place, Faye. Please."

"No. I want you to see for yourself what the lesbian life is like. You'll understand better if you do. Here you can *see* why I can't marry you."

She ran her fingers down the side of the bottle, digging at the wet-soft label. "You mean more to me than anybody, Gene," she said. She rolled the paper into a ball. "Do you know that?"

"Yes."

Her eyes were shiningly wet now, fixed on Gene with a sadness, both futile and tender. Her gaze was so powerful that he could hardly tear his own eyes from her.

He glanced across the room finally to a booth against the far wall. Faye's eyes followed his. Two women were in the booth, sitting side by side. As Gene and Faye watched, one of the women, dressed in slacks and very masculine looking, put her hand up the dress of the other woman. Both were drunk.

Gene's cheeks burned with embarrassment. He turned back to look at Faye.

"You see," she said. "That's what I want Mickey to do to me." Her bottom lip began to tremble, and in a second sobs were tumbling out of her, her whole face a tight-drawn mask.

Gene reached out for her.

He did not see the woman come out of the crowd at the bar and start toward them. With his eyes on Faye he saw nothing but her face as it turned slowly to him, afraid and pleading and asking him, please, to understand, please, oh God, Gene, please.

"Faye."

He touched her, he let his fingers go around her waist, hard and gripping, telling her in his squeeze that he was here, still here, always here.

"I haven't done anything, Gene," she blurted. "You got to believe me, I haven't done anything..." her voice cracked weakly, "...with a woman. I'm not sure that I'm all the way les. I just think so. I want to try it, though...with a woman. I want a woman. That's what's wrong with me, I'm going crazy with it, wanting a woman all the time."

Then the hand on her shoulder, and Gene looked up.

Mickey Jessup smirked down at Faye. She was dressed in slacks and a shirt and tie. Her hair was combed flat-back, mannishly.

"It took you long enough to get around," she said to Faye. She glanced at Gene. "Hi, Little Boy Blue. What are you doing in *here*? The place for queer men is down the street. I know; that's where all my husbands ended up."

"Let's go," Gene said to Faye.

"Go? You just got here. Aren't you going to ask me to sit down?" Mickey's face was glitterishly alive. "I'm sitting next to young Miss Sherritt, though. I don't go for phonies like you," she said to Gene. "Playing man when all the time you're mooning over Mark. Come on, ask me to sit down. I dare you. I'll show you what can be done with a delicious dish like Miss Sherritt."

Gene was sick with weakness and fright; then in almost a panic he wanted to jump up and run, but he was too afraid, too weak, to even do that. First Faye's, then Mickey's talk of all his feelings toward Mark had graphically drawn, had torn the surface, what he had felt only vaguely and uncomfortably before.

"What's the matter, did I say something naughty?" Mickey cooed. "You know, something true."

Gene could only sit like a robot and fight to keep his eyes on Mickey, fight to keep up an insulted front. He didn't trust himself to use words. Then he felt Faye's stare and he glanced at her, and in her eyes he saw that she agreed with Mickey.

"We're going now," Faye finally said to Mickey her expression tearing at her face.

She had moved to the edge of the seat toward Mickey, as if to stop her from sitting down.

"I want to talk to you before you leave, Faye," Mickey said, almost commanding.

"I don't have time."

"Come on back to the little girls' room with me."

"No."

Then Gene heard Mickey say, "Faye," low and intense and commanding, and look, stare-deep, into Faye's eyes.

Faye swung away from Mickey's probing gaze and looked at Gene, her eyes imploring him for help.

"Let's go," Gene managed. He moved to get up.

But Faye was staring back at Mickey now, her eyes, uncontrollably, it seemed fixed on the woman.

"Let's go in the back, Faye," Mickey intoned. Her voice was quietly strong and controlled.

Then Faye was moving on the seat and was going up to Mickey, mechanically, as if hypnotized by Mickey's eyes, her glitterish strong eyes pulling on Faye, magnetizing Faye, an expression on Faye's face that went icicling into Gene. Up to Mickey she went.

Going away from Gene, her expression numb and helpless.

And Gene sat, lips zippered, nailed to the table, and watched her go. Then something broke in him; something exploded and shattered his inertia, his fear; something that Mark had been trying to tell him for weeks: to go after Faye.

"Faye," he said. Go after Faye, his new strength said. Go after Faye, Mark had said.

She had not heard him call her name; it had not snapped her fusion with Mickey. She was following Mickey toward the rear of the building.

"Faye!"

She stopped at his voice, and turned, hesitating. Then, trance-like, she went on after Mickey.

Go after Faye!

Gene sprang up. Through tables and chairs and staring, grinning women he went after Faye. He caught her and grabbed her and held on to her arm.

"Faye, honey, come on out with me."

She was trembling in his arms, leaning against him, anguish and misery in her eyes.

"Oh, Gene."

Then he was leading her toward the door. She began to sob and her mind came back into her face. "God, oh God," wet streaming down her cheeks. "My God, my God," and she stumbled once and almost fell, but Gene caught her and they went outside into the car. "Oh, God, what am I going to do?"

Gene gunned the car away from the Intimate, away from the sick and the twisted; blindly, he drove Faye home.

At her front door, when he tried to kiss her, she drew back.

"No," she said.

"Faye."

He tried to pull her close, but she held him away.

"Please, Faye."

"It's no use. Why get yourself excited?"

"Kiss me."

"You've got the wrong sex tonight," she mumbled. She turned to go in.

"See you tomorrow?"

She shrugged. "Kind of silly, don't you think?"

"I'll phone you," he said.

"I don't want you to phone me anymore, Gene. I can't see you anymore. For your own good."

"Faye."

"It's for your own good, don't you see?"

"No," he said.

But she went into the house. She was crying when she closed the door.

CHAPTER THIRTEEN

Gene went down to Mark's the next evening. He went into the living room and sat down alone with Mark, holding the man's arm, and went into Faye, telling Mark everything, unclogging himself, Mark nodding knowing, nodding, saying, Go After Faye. He knew Faye, Mark said; he knew what must be done. He, Gene, must go after Faye; she needed and had to have someone to shoulder her problems, someone to stand with—and maybe even on. And if the someone wasn't a man, it would be a woman, Mark warned. Go After Faye. Stop piddling around. Go After Faye.

Go after Faye. But since she had told him what she suspected about herself, and since he had had time to think about it, Gene wasn't at all sure he now wanted to go after Faye. And the reason for this feeling to want to retreat from her was more than that she was a mixed-up person who would now give him pain; after all, she had always been mixed-up, had always given him pain, and he had kept coming back for more. The reason lay below. The reason was somehow connected to the fact that he had, just now, thought of her, not as a woman, but as a person.

There was only one thing he didn't mention, or even think about, as he talked to Mark. What Mickey and Faye had accused him of feeling toward Mark was a laughing thing now. When he had felt close to Mark, when Mark had touched him and he had wanted to return the touch, he had thought it was a womanlike pull. It was simply Mark saying to him, Go after Faye. He had been drawn to Mark because through Mark, out of Mark, came the command, Go after Faye, which he needed as a push, a fatherlike order that told him it was the right thing to go after Faye. Gene was like a little boy and Mark was like a father—a strong, commanding father that Gene had needed and had never had.

Go after Faye, and Gene left Mark's and started making habit-turns toward Faye's house. So easy, the ride to Faye's. So natural. Each turn so well known. Each traffic light. Each bump, each crack in the street. The route was long-grooved in memory, part of him, like Faye, like the habit of her presence, like her buoyancy and her weight and her closeness, and now, like her absence.

He glanced at the vacant seat beside him.

"Hi," he said.

His chuckle went sour; and in sagging thoughts he drove on to Faye's house.

It was a little before ten when he went by her home. Her room was dark, in contrast to the downstairs lights. He drove around the block and parked far enough away from her door so that she would not see him when she came in, yet close enough so that he could see her when she walked up to her front porch.

He waited, watching the glow of one cigarette, then another, and the headlights of passing cars on his wristwatch.

Ten-thirty. No Faye.

Bo came home, bursting up to the house in a jalopy that bulged with teenagers. She ran in behind a chorus of goodnights. The front door slammed, the jalopy roared off.

Gene lit a match and looked at his watch again. Quarter of eleven.

House lights flashed off one by one, and Gene yawned.

And jerked upright on the seat. A figure under a street light. It turned a corner and started down the sidewalk toward Faye's house. The light silhouetted the outlines of a coat, the shape of a head. A woman. Her walk was a sluggish drag, her shoulders humped, her face bent toward the pavement. It was Faye.

She was at her front walk when Gene called out to her. His voice startled him; it was so loud and crisp against the sleeping house, strangely incongruous.

He saw her stop in her front yard. She turned and watched him walk rapidly toward her.

"Hi," he made himself snap.

"Gene," she murmured, happily surprised.

He let his hands slide in under arms, and she leaned against him.

"Faye," he whispered, pulling her close. "Oh, Faye, I wanted to see you so bad." He felt her trembling, her face cold on his neck.

"Faye, please," he mumbled. He felt her tighten in next to him. "You got to see a psychiatrist."

Her head moved on his cheek in negative shakes. "It's no use," she whimpered.

"Don't talk like that."

"Besides, it takes money."

"I'll pay for it. Somehow."

She drew her head from his shoulder, her face shadowed in the moonlight. "I don't want anybody fooling around with my mind."

She began to cry. "There's only one thing I want to do," she sobbed.

Gene waited. There was anguish and misery and disgust in her voice, and he was afraid to ask her what it was she wanted to do.

"Oh, Gene," she moaned, burrowing her face into his neck, embarrassed and ashamed. "I feel so dirty. So filthy."

She moaned again.

"I'm no good. I'm worse than a whore."

He felt her fingers dig into his arm, tighten, tighten.

"All I want to do is go see Shim," she sobbed, the words tearing at her, like sandpaper scraping her raw. "Just watch her, her body, the way she does that act."

"Faye."

"Just watch a dirty stripteaser, that's all I want to do. It's driving me crazy, just wanting and wanting to see her. You got to take me back there, Gene. You got to." She broke away from him, fright and horror in her eyes. "I got to find out what this is all about. What makes me want to look at her and..." her voice crumbled; she pushed her head against Gene's chest "...want to sleep with her." She sobbed, terrible and agonized. "Oh, Gene, Gene."

"You can't see her again, Faye, you can't. You'll just stir up all those feelings, watching her."

She shook her head in quick negative jerks. "No! When I see her, it satisfies me. I don't want her anymore, afterwards. For a while." Her fingers squeezed into his back. "Now all I do is *think* and *think* about her. It's like a disease, like wanting dope. You got to take me to see her, Gene. You *got* to."

"I can't," he mumbled. "I can't sit there and watch you, the way you look at her." His head jerked. "I can't!"

She quieted; she pushed herself away and she would not look at him.

"I'll go alone, then." Her voice was dry and hollow.

"Faye." He reached out for her; she was going toward the porch.

"I'm sorry," she mumbled. "I can't help myself."

"No, Faye."

But she turned and went quickly into the house.

CHAPTER FOURTEEN

As soon as Gene drove away, Faye came quietly out of the house. She walked away from her home until she reached a main drag two blocks away. She caught a cab. "Drive toward Chicago," she told the driver. "I'll tell you where to let me off."

Riding toward the city, Faye breathed at an excited pitch. Every few miles she caressed the inside of her leg, moaning softly, despairingly. When the cab reached the nightspot where she and Gene had seen Shim, she got out of the taxi. She went into the club and sat at a table as close to the floor as she could get.

She watched the monotony of the preliminary hip-grinding, breast-swishing, sex-swishing with a bored expression, disinterested. She wanted only to see Shim.

When the assorted nakedness had been shown, the band flared, subsided, a spotlight came on and the same emaciated MC mince-stepped onto the floor and introduced Shim. The woman came onto the floor, dressed in her half-man, half-woman clothes. The lights lowered, the music slid low and crawling, and she went into her self-seduction pantomime. Faye's face became intense, both in fascination and horror, as if she were being drawn to the woman even though the sight of the dancer sickened her. Faye watched the whole self-seduction, half-and-half act without touching her drink. When it was over she nervously asked the headwaiter if she could go back to Shim's dressing room. The man went to the room, then came back and told Faye it was okay.

When Faye got back to the small dressing room, Shim was sitting by herself in front of a mirror, just beginning to take off her makeup. She was still dressed in her half-man, half-woman clothes.

"What do you want, baby?" she said in a masculine voice. She was a woman in her early thirties, tough-looking but attractive. Her body was curved but not deeply so.

"I...I...I just wanted to meet you," Faye stammered. "I want to tell you I liked your dance very much."

"I saw you at the table out there. How come you all alone, baby? Beautiful as you are, I'd think men would be swarming over you. Don't you like 'em, baby?" Her smile was provocative.

"Ah...my boyfriend's sick."

"Yeah? You mean you're tired of him, don't you?"

"Well..."

"Sit down," Shim said, patting the seat beside her in front of the mirror. "Let's talk it over. I get a lot of girls in here like you."

Faye felt excitement surge through her as she sat next to Shim and felt the woman's leg press against hers. She looked into the mirror and saw the dancer's suggestive smile. When Shim's arm went around her, she began to pant.

"Excited, honey?" Shim purred.

"No," she said weakly.

"What do you want, honey? Me?"

"No..." Faye began, but her voice broke when Shim bent close to her and brushed her ear with her lips.

"Baby, baby, you're beautiful," Shim murmured, her voice husky. "I like you, baby. I want you bad."

Quickly then, Shim got up and locked the dressing room door. She sat beside Faye again. Her hand glided up and down Faye's leg. Faye could hardly breathe, she was so excited. Shim was a person who exactly fitted what Faye wanted in sex. Shim—dressed as she was—was neither a man nor a woman. She was both, some of each. She was like Faye, who felt like a woman sometimes, like a man other times.

When Faye felt Shim's hot breath in her ear, she saw in the mirror the side of Shim's face that was made up like a woman. Then, as Shim stood and went behind Faye and cupped Faye's breasts with her hands, Shim turned her face the other way so that Faye could see the dancer's male side. Then, looking in the mirror as Shim stood up straight behind the seated Faye, Faye could see both the man and woman side of makeup and dress.

Faye felt a hot fire in her that made her gasp and moan. She had never felt such desire before. She wanted Shim to take her completely; she wanted the dancer to do everything possible to her.

Faye felt Shim's hands once again cup her twin mounds of hot flesh. Then the dancer's fingers slipped down inside of Faye's dress, slowly dropping down, feeling, caressing. Faye rose off the seat, moaning.

"Now, baby, now," moaned Shim. Faye felt the dancer's body press against her back.

"Oh," said Faye, "don't stop."

Faye let Shim undress her. Then Shim undressed. And immediately, seeing Shim without her half-man, half-woman clothes on, Faye's interest slackened. Without her queer clothes on, Shim became more of a woman, and thus, Faye was not attracted as much. She still desired the dancer, though, and when Shim took her to a couch in the dressing room, Faye went eagerly.

Later, she pushed Shim away and sat up. Weakly she got dressed and left the club. She got a taxi and, exhausted, headed back toward Chelsor. But even as tired as she was she could not sleep on the way home. She began to feel horribly depressed and guilty. Every time she thought of what she had just done, waves of embarrassment and guilt washed over her.

About halfway home she had another hallucination. She thought she saw Shim sitting naked beside her in the taxi. She screamed. The white-faced cab driver stopped the car and wanted to know what was wrong. But the scream brought her back to her senses. "Nothing," she told the driver. "It's okay. I was just dreaming." She rode the rest of the way home quietly, although she was so depressed that all she could think of was going to sleep and never waking up again.

But later she came to the decision that she must get professional help.

CHAPTER FIFTEEN

Go after Faye. Go after Faye. The words hammered at Gene. But lurking in his mind was the question of whom he was going after. Go after Faye. But who was Faye? Go after whom? Who was she? And his thinking stumbled over the use of the word she. Was she a woman or a man?

Yet, when the phone rang the next day and he heard Faye's voice, little quivering puffballs bounced in him and sang, Go After Faye.

"Gene," she said, her voice barely audible, "were you serious about that psychiatrist last night? About paying for it, I mean?"

"Of course I was serious," he answered softly.

"I went to see one this morning."

His fingers tightened around the receiver.

"I phoned him early and he told me to come right over. It's going to cost a lot, Gene."

"I'll get you the money."

"And I'll pay you back."

His fingers were still tight around the receiver, waiting for the caress of more words.

"You were right about going to see a psychiatrist. I feel better already."

"You don't feel half as good as I do." The words were choking him; they wouldn't come out evenly nicely and without restraint. "Everything's going to be all right," he said.

"I hope so," she murmured.

"Oh, Faye, I could sing."

She chuckled self-consciously. "See you tonight?" she whispered.

"Yes," he said. "Yes."

As he started to put the receiver down, he suddenly blurted, "Faye!"

"Huh?"

"I'm so glad, Faye."

"So am I."

But she had hesitated too long; and her voice was fumbly and unsure.

She remained fumbly and unsure when she first started seeing the psychiatrist. But as time and treatment began to take effect she responded, she brightened, with occasional relapses.

She'd come out from the doctor's residence—a snug bungalow, sedate and evergreened, which served both as his home and office—and get into Gene's car.

"How did it go tonight?" he'd ask, trying to grin, forcing lightness into his voice.

She smiled where before she shrugged. "Okay," she said, where earlier in the treatment she would have mumbled, "The same," slumped on the seat, moody and silent.

She changed gradually. Her change from the night when she was beginning treatment and they took the "just riding" way home and she asked Gene why he was paying for "all this stuff when I'm a hopeless case," and he had tried to laugh a little but his voice was stringy and weak—her change from this to, later, when they took the "just riding" way home and they parked and talked and laughed, wrapped up snug in the warmth of each other.

Her change from the night when he took her home and she said she doubted if she'd keep seeing the psychiatrist anymore because "I'm getting worse," to the night when she said she doubted she'd see the doctor much longer, at least so steadily, because "he says I'm doing fine."

And her change from the night when she got out of her bed and lay down on the floor in front of the open window where it was cold and hard and she would not think about seeing Shim—her change from the hell of this to sleeping all night without nightmares of Shims or fathers screaming drunkenly at her.

And behind her change, with the change, pushing the change—and sometimes pushing himself—was Gene and his Go After Faye.

Her change from avoiding people to the night she instigated and kept going and was a part, a slam-bang affair with smiling, bright people that slam-banged its way through an evening at an apartment of a married couple Faye knew and hadn't kept in contact with for years. A group that grinningly encouraged Faye in her climb back to her role as a happy, well-adjusted woman.

Exuberantly she cornered Gene in the kitchen. "It's working," she laughed. "It's working, Gene. I'm coming out of it." Then she kissed him quickly and hurried back into the living room, murmuring, "Just like old times—only now I've got you."

Then, toward the end, she put her hand in his, tightening it when she felt his responsive grip.

"Hi," he said.

She turned and quickly kissed him.

"Hi yourself," and she kissed him again. "Let's go as soon as we can," she murmured, an urgency now in her voice, a suggestion.

After coffee and sandwiches they left the party and went out and got into Gene's car. Before Faye had closed the door she was in his arms.

"I'm okay," she said. "It's gone. I can even say the word perversion. It's gone. It's gone, Gene," and she was burying herself into him. "It's gone. I'm okay."

She broke away from him then, slowly, deliberately. Her face was shining like a new sun, throwing more light than the light from a lamppost nearby. Then, something like humbleness came out along with the sun, and came out, too, with her voice, the words both proud and humble:

"Please, Gene, if you want to, let's sleep together to-night."

She came back into him and crept inside his arms.

"Please, Gene. Please. I'm okay now. It's okay, it's gone. Not feeling that way. It's you now. It's you and me. I want you tonight. I want to love you tonight, all night. Please. Tonight, Gene. I want to. I have to. Please help me, Gene."

"Faye."

"I've never felt like this before. I mean, it's like all of me wants you now, not like it used to be, just part of me. Oh, Gene, I want to get in bed with you, feel you next to me, close, all of you and all of me. I don't know, I don't know." Her fingers were digging into his arms. "I don't know if I want you the way I ought to, but I think I do. I mean, I have to find out. I've never been like other girls. I've got to find out on my own, by myself." A sound like a whimper flowed from her. "And if it doesn't work tonight—the way I feel, wanting to try so bad—it never will."

"Oh, Faye, sweet."

But his voice was hesitant; now it was he who was fumbly and unsure.

"Just with you, Gene. I could never do it with another man. You won't hurt me. I know you won't hurt me. It will be bad for me if you hurt me."

"No hurting. There won't be any hurting."

"Please, Gene, let's go."

He was stepping on the starter.

"I've got to try tonight. Like a woman."

He moved the car away from the curb. But he was uneasy, and he didn't want to go. He didn't want to go to bed with Faye. He realized now he was not attracted to her that way, even if he had been before.

CHAPTER SIXTEEN

They drove directly to his apartment. Inside, Gene started to turn on the living room light. He wanted to talk to Faye; he wanted to postpone; he wanted to avoid; he almost wanted to run. But Faye was in his arms before he could reach the switch. Then, quickly, she led him to the bedroom her fingers tight on his hand. "Please, Gene," tugging at him, crumbling him so that when they were in the dark bedroom and Faye was taking off her clothes and standing naked to him, waiting, wanting, he was in an agony of conflicts, and he didn't yet undress.

Faye came to him, hesitantly, then strongly, walking like a naked dream across the room to take him into her arms, the soft silk of her giving body pressed tight against him.

"Please, Gene, now."

"In a minute," he said.

"Should I have waited for you? You have to tell me, Gene. You have to tell me what to do." Her voice was mounting again.

"You did right," he said.

"Please, Gene, take your clothes off. Why don't you? Why don't you, Gene?"

"I am," he said.

He broke from her and fumbled to the bed and sat down and began to take off his shoes.

"Gene?"

"Yes?"

"I know why you're holding back. Don't tell me, I don't want to talk about it now. But I know. I want you to know that I know. I can help you too. Like you're helping me."

"No, it's not that. I know what you mean."

"We won't talk about it now," she said. "Later."

"Yes."

No, they would not talk about it later. He would never tell her why he was hesitant. What was she thinking was wrong? It was something else. And he couldn't tell her what it was because it would grind her back into the mire and dirty her again and maybe she would never be able to ever get out.

"Gene?" she said, sitting beside him and nestling her fingers in his hair.

"Yes?"

"It's so dark. I think it's better when it's dark, don't you? Is that the way other girls feel?"

She was like a little girl, and he almost wanted to cry, and because of this he quickly undressed and lifted her into his lap as if she were a baby.

"Gene," she murmured, "I'm going to try so hard, but you have to help me."

"Yes."

"Try, Gene."

Then they lay down beside each other and she was saying, "Don't hurt me, Gene. Please. It will be bad if you do—for me."

"There won't be any hurt," he said, and immediately he thought, he must go through with it, he must force himself. To leave her would be to hurt her terribly. He must force himself, although all he wanted to do now was go.

Her arms were around his neck now, and they were side by side with her lips nuzzled in against his cheek. She started to talk, little-girl words whimpering out of her, her arms tight around him, pulling herself in givingly close, words clinging to his ears and mind, words afraid and excited and pleading.

"Gene, honey, oh Gene. You're so good to me. So patient. I'm going to try so hard. Let me kiss you. Gene. Kiss me some more. Kiss me some more, Gene, don't stop. Are you supposed to stop now? Yes, keep your hand there. There, yes. Yes, I like that. Yes, Gene. Isn't that right? Like this?"

"Yes."

"Gene?"

"Yes."

"I don't want to yet. I don't want you all the way yet. I've wanted you before." She whimpered. "Why don't I want you now?"

"You will," he said. I won't, he thought. "Takes time," he said.

"Is that the truth? Tell me the truth, Gene."

"Sh-sh."

"It shouldn't take so much time. You got to tell me the truth."

"It does."

"I'm trying, Gene. I'm trying."

"Sh-sh."

"I want to talk to you. I feel like talking to you."

Now she was pulling him to her, awkwardly, with tugs and jerks at his back, pushing herself against him, squirming with desperate shoves.

She whimpered again.

"Sh-sh."

"It must be that stripteaser, that Shim thing."

"Don't talk about her."

"I can't help it."

"You have to forget her."

"I can't help it."

"You have to forget her."

"Oh, Gene, I feel awful."

"Honey."

"Let's start now," she said. "Anyway."

"No. I'll hurt you."

"I don't care. Tell me what you want me to do. I want to help. I want to do it right."

It was awkward and fumbly and she was wanting to help so frantically, her "I can do it" so eager, her "Is that right?" so tenderly violent, so pitiful that he wanted only to hold her, little-girl close, and just go to sleep with her protectively in his arms.

"Gene, what's the matter? You're stopping."

"I'm hurting you," he lied.

"No, it's all right. Go on. Don't stop. Please. You mustn't.

"Faye."

"Gene," she said, "don't stop. Why are you stopping?"

"Faye, honey, I..."

"Gene, what are you getting up for? Where are you going? Gene, what's the matter!" he heard her whisper, her voice like the sound of a moan.

The matter, he thought when his feet were on the floor, was the months of knowing Faye Sherritt. The matter of carrying the weight of her problems, and yes, the matter of the joy, too, he had had in being able to carry her problems, or at least try to. The matter of from the very beginning being attracted to Faye Sherritt, yet at the same time of being wary and sometimes even afraid of her. The matter was the memory, the memory that had caught up with him and had become now.

The matter, Faye Sherritt, is you.

But only after a moment's hesitation, he added: And me.

The matter of wanting and waiting for her and now to have her, to have her wanting him, and he not to want her. The matter of not being able to tell her why. Wanting her desperately up until the time he realized she might be an out-and-out homosexual.

He had not realized how he felt when—with this new realization—and afterwards had not stopped to analyze the vague change in his feelings toward her, how he had grown to think of her less as a wanted woman and more as a friend in need, less of her as his girl, and more of her as a person—a person in trouble. His rush to help her and her dependence on him had blinded the nature of his change in feelings.

The matter was simply that he had come to think of her—unconsciously until now—as a man. And thinking of her as a man he did not want her sexually.

And, of course, he couldn't tell her how he thought of her; to tell her he thought of her as a man would undermine all the fight-toward-womanhood that she had accomplished.

But now a new thought in his present arena of exposed thoughts came charging to the surface: If he did not want her, thinking she was a man, then he must be okay, a normal man. If he was not attracted to manlike Faye then he was normal in his sexual life, an area of himself that had bothered him, with no concrete reason, for years, and more recently in the fact that he had been attracted, more than usually he had thought until he understood the reason, to Mark and to a non-feminine woman such as Faye. He had even, at first, been attracted to mannish Mickey, until he discovered that she was too mannish, too tough. It must be, he mused, that he had enough woman in him to be attracted to a non-feminine type woman such as Faye—and that was why he was attracted, and continued to be, to her in the first place—but not enough feminine in him to be attracted to a man.

And with the thought his face and thinking lightened and he began to be conscious of Faye, numb and hurtingly silent, lying behind him on the bed.

Damn it, he spat at the thinking end of himself, Faye's no man. She's a healthy, wanting woman—confused and neurotic, true, as he was and had been; that was another reason they had joined forces—who had climbed out of her swamp with his help. And now, through his own confused thinking and feeling, he had typed the label MAN on her and used it as a proof, for his own benefit, of his own normality.

Well, he didn't need proof, and he didn't need labels, and he didn't need any more thoughts. Faye was with him, waiting, wanting, and that was all that he needed. He turned to her. He went to her.

Faye, lying on the bed alone like an icicle left by itself when all the others have been meltingly warmed, saw him coming. She had lain these last few minutes in a terror that spun thoughts through her in a mad whirl. Grinding her was the belief that Gene had left her because he thought he was not all man, that he couldn't go through with love-making because he was, or thought he was, homosexual himself.

Two reasons now she had for praying that he would turn and come to her just once more: to prove to herself that she was a woman and to prove to Gene that he was a man.

And when he turned and came to her again she was almost cryingly weak with relief and thanks, and she had to swallow hard to keep tears from running into his lips where he kissed her, so passionately, so desperately wanting that she was giving, and taking, before she knew there was any hurting involved. "Oh," she said, "oh," and he was murmuring sweet syrupy words to her, her ears like flowers to honey them in, her mouth like a cup to catch him, to fill him and herself.

Afterwards, the joy and even more, and they knew it would never stop, because now they both could make it go!

—THE END—

WHAT MAD PURSUIT?
An Editor's Afterword to John D. Keefauver's *Tormented Virgin*

SCOTT NICOLAY

John D. Keefauver was one of fiction's last great free-lancers, and throughout his long literary career he kept meticulous files of all his manuscripts and detailed records of all his sales. Two of the earliest entries in his sales journal document checks from Art Enterprises, Inc. on April 5 and April 11, 1962. The first was for $500.00, and the second only $50. Given the publisher, the date, and the amounts relative to his other sales from that time, these almost certainly represent payments Keefauver received for *Tormented Virgin*. He made only a single reference to that novel elsewhere in his files: the annotation "Tor. Vir?" scrawled near the top of a typed list of eight novels he had written by 1989.

Outside of these few brief notes and his name on the book's cover and title page, nothing else survives to tie Keefauver to his longest published work. Visitors to his Carmel apartment recall seeing his personal copy of the lurid little volume, heavily annotated and with certain pages removed, but neither that copy nor the original manuscript remained among his papers after his death. The text of *Tormented Virgin* is one of only two known published works missing from his files. Sadly, the other is his earliest major sale, the poem "Oh Well, What the Hell," a parody of

Lawrence Ferlinghetti's "Coney Island of the Mind" that appeared in the November 1958 issue of *Playboy*.

Once I took on the responsibility of editing Keefauver's work for posthumous publication, it became my grail quest to find the original typescript of *Tormented Virgin*, or failing that, the author's marked-up copy of the published book. Obviously I would have liked access to any corrections, edits, or other annotations he might have made to either version, but I wanted above all to read the novel's ending as Keefauver originally wrote it, and to see what notes he might have written or inserted *in the final pages* of that cheap little paperback whose cover bears only the most general resemblance to its contents (we have at least been able to improve on that aspect with a beautiful new cover by James O'Barr).[1] I am a poor Percival alas, and both those copies of the text appear lost forever, along with any possible alternate "original" ending.

I refer to an "original" ending because I am not convinced the published version is Keefauver's first take. As Brit Mandelo points out in their insightful introduction to this edition of *Tormented Virgin*, the ending as we have it "doesn't ring particularly true." Not only does that ending not ring true for these characters or their story—as Mandelo makes clear—*it does not ring true for Keefauver*. Having by now probably read as much or more of his work than anyone else currently living, I can make that statement with some confidence. For one thing, Keefauver loved a twist ending, and he loved it from the start of his long career. Though he does not always go the full

O. Henry, virtually every piece of fiction he wrote concludes with some kind of twist, surprise, or clever wordplay. Not all of his endings hold up today, but the published finale of *Tormented Virgin* does not feel like Keefauver at all. It feels forced, artificial, and simply flat. Most of all, it feels tacked on. In fact, I think the tack marks still show, and not only at the novel's end.

In the last chapter of *Tormented Virgin*, just as Faye and Gene seem poised for the consummation the book has teased for so long, the narrative suddenly switches from dialogue (peppered with increasingly titillating stage directions) back to prose. Chapter Sixteen is almost entirely a repeat of Chapter One, even using most of the same language, so by this point it becomes clear that the flash-forward at the novel's opening was a preview of its end. The pivotal moment of this modest literary ouroboros comes after these two lines revealing Gene's internal monologue:

> *The matter, Faye Sherrit, is you.*
> *But only after a moment's hesitation, he added: And me.*

This passage echoes the end of the first chapter, with only slight changes:

> *The matter, he thought, is you.*
> *But after only a moment's hesitation, he added, and me.*

The miniature *Finnegans Wake* loop around which this salacious little novel has taken us ends here, and everything that follows feels false. The "resolution" that recenters heterosexual norms is unsatisfying even as fiction. The remaining prose comes across as rushed and stilted, and the twist ending that marks virtually all Keefauver's published fiction is missing altogether.

I could be wrong. In the early Sixties when Keefauver sold this novel to Art Enterprises, Inc., he was just beginning his literary career. Much of his best work was still a decade or more in the future. Could it be that the ending of *Tormented Virgin* was the best he could do at the time, that he was simply unable to do justice to the bisexual attractions that fill the novel's entire narrative arc until its last three pages?

Keefauver's writing in chapters 2-15 suggests otherwise. Though pulp fiction prose, much of it achieves the sort of gritty realism that hits the medium's sweet spot. Keefauver's ideas about gender and sexuality may be painfully cis, het, and just plain dated, but at its best, as in the awkward scenes between the four principal characters, the writing in *Tormented Virgin* compares favorably to some of the better pulp novels published by comparable houses during that period. Charles Willeford's *Pick-Up* and *The Woman Chaser* offer particularly good comparisons. The aforementioned poetic parody Keefauver published four years earlier in *Playboy* is strong enough to stand up to Ferlinghetti's original. The available evidence suggests that his writing chops, if not at their peak when he wrote *Tormented Virgin*, were already developed enough to craft an ending with a little more zing than the one with which he left us.

Keefauver cut his writing teeth as a journalist, following an American literary tradition established by Hemingway, Crane, and Bierce before him. Gene Bond, the agonized protagonist of *Tormented Virgin*, is also a reporter. The Chelsor *Press*, the fictional paper where Gene and most of the novel's other characters are employed, is obviously based on the former *Herald Press* (now the *Herald-Palladium*) of St. Joseph's, Michigan, where Keefauver worked in 1953. How much Gene himself is based on the author is hard to say, but many of the leads in his later work—characters such as Cutliffe Starkvogel, and Uncle Coleslaw, and the ubiquitous Henry J. Littlefinger—are obvious surrogates for the author. Perhaps some of the other dramatis personae of *Tormented Virgin* were based at least partly on Keefauver's former coworkers, but prying into that history would be a bridge too far.

It is easy however, to picture Keefauver's publishers calling him from their office at 8511 Sunset Boulevard to tell him that the original ending of *Tormented Virgin* would "have to go" in order to appeal to their straight male readership. Easy to picture a seedy smutlord simulacrum of J. Jonah Jameson chewing a cigar as he chewed Keefauver out. We know from Charles Nuetzel and others who have written about working for operations on a par with Art Enterprises, Inc. that their editors did indeed demand major revisions to fit their formulae (formulae that required a sex scene every twenty pages, for instance). Easy as well to see Keefauver knocking out a quick couple pages and tacking them on, then rewriting the final chapter (or maybe just marking up a carbon of it) to serve as a new opening and to reframe the altered end. Probably an extra paragraph to segue into the beginning of what then became Chapter Two.

It is easy to picture all that, but alas, without Keefauver's typescript or other notes, we will never know. Of course none of this conjecture gives us any idea how Keefauver might have ended *Tormented Virgin* if he had complete freedom to do so any way he wanted. That any such alternate ending ever existed might be only wishful thinking on my part, the desire to believe a major early work by a writer I have admired since my childhood lived up to the storytelling bar set by his best tales.

One last indirect but important line of evidence for editorial changes to *Tormented Virgin* deserves consideration. The market for cheap pulp and erotic paperbacks remained strong well into the Sixties, and John D. Keefauver was not the only writer to work there who later went on to more respectable markets. Crime writers such as Charles Willeford, Harry Whittington, and Charles Williams published novels under their own names with presses inhabiting the same shady literary ecology as Art Enterprises. Science fiction writers in particular seem to have thrived in those markets: Robert Silverberg published hundreds of softcore novels as "Don Elliot" and other *noms-de-plume*, Andrew L. Offutt made an entire secret career of it, and Jack Jardine (Agents of T.E.R.R.A.) actually worked for Art Enterprises and thus may have been one of Keefauver's editors under his Larry Maddock/Maddox pseudonym. However, as prolific a writer as Keefauver was, he does not appear to have written any other paperbacks for the softcore market. Nor does any evidence exist to suggest he ever worked under another name, either in that market or any other. He did, however, go on to publish extensively in the men's magazines of his time, and became a regular contributor to *Playboy's* "Ribald Classics" column, so he obviously had no problem with such content. His work continued to feature erotic themes and elements throughout his career.

If Keefauver experienced editorial interference with the ending of *Tormented Virgin*, it might explain why he abandoned a market that could have proven lucrative for him at the time. The only other "novel" he published during his lifetime was *The Three Day Traffic Jam* in 1992, an 89-page middle-grade treatment of a theme he returned to multiple times in his fiction, including several of his best short stories.

This was not for lack of trying, however. At least half a dozen unpublished novels survive in Keefauver's files. The stack of his correspondence with agents and publishers regarding the earliest of these, *Noodles* (AKA *Mr. Noodles*), is as thick as the novel itself, and he came painfully close to placing it several times. According to a list of his finished novels he typed up in 1989, *Noodles* was completed by 1959, several years before he published *Tormented Virgin*. This chronology suggests he may already have set his sights on the mainstream fiction market by the time he sold the latter novel to Art Enterprises, in which case it may simply have been a fluke, perhaps a one-off opportunity to make some quick cash.

Alas, the mainstream market never opened its doors to John D. Keefauver the novelist, which leaves *Tormented Virgin* occupying a position in his legacy he probably did not anticipate in 1962. If he could have foreseen this would be his only published novel, he might have made some different choices regarding its publication. He might have pursued a more reputable publisher, or even withheld the novel from print altogether. He might also have delivered a longer, more developed story.[2] And of course, there is that ending. Although a better finish could have put this book on a level with Willeford or Whittington, I agree with Brit Mandelo that it is a stretch to imagine a version where Faye, Gene, Mickey, Mark, and perhaps even Shim all "get together." Such an ending could have validated the bisexual desire and polyamory at the heart of the novel, but whether Keefauver was ever truly prepared to take these themes to the conclusion they deserved is doubtful. Nonetheless, based on my knowledge of the rest of Keefauver's corpus, published and unpublished, I remain convinced he must once have written something in between the potential manifesto for the sexual revolution this novel could have delivered and the forced show of conformity it hands us in the end.

What we are left with is an artifact that deserves rescue from literary oblivion primarily for its "unintentionally provocative" character, as Brit Mandelo so expertly frames it. Keefauver may be pointing toward the fences in *Tormented Virgin*, but he never got the ball out of the infield. Within those limitations, however, he gave us a work whose interrogation of its own historical context, like the narrative playing out on Keats' urn, defies resolution: "Heard melodies are sweet, but those unheard / Are sweeter." The obvious artificiality of the novel's conclusion only accentuates this tension, even as it generates questions we can no longer answer about Keefauver, his process, and the text itself.

___

FOR FURTHER READING:

Charles Nuetzell, *Pocketbook Writer: Confessions of a Commercial Hack.* Wildside Press, 2008
Chris Offutt, *My Father, the Pornographer: A Memoir.* Washington Square Press, 2017

___

[1] The original 1962 cover of *Tormented Virgin* is a direct copy of a painting of Eva Lynd by artist Mike Ludlow that appeared in the Sept. 7, 1957 *Saturday Evening Post*. Lynd also modeled for many of the "Men's Adventure" magazines which occupied a niche during that era barely above the most of the stuff Art Enterprises published. Ludlow was a well-known pinup artist in his time who also painted the cover art for a whole series of mildly salacious Dell paperbacks in the late Fifties. Whether the anonymous cover artist for *Tormented Virgin* stole from Ludlow, or may have been Ludlow himself, slumming during a period when he was losing much of his steady work to photographers, remains another mystery.

[2] One possible interpretation of the cryptic notes on Keefauver's 1989 novel list is that *Tormented Virgin* is a version of his lost "College Park era" novel. His notes record this as finished in 1952, and "shortened in 1961." If that is the case, Keefauver wrote the

original story *before* he moved to Michigan and revised it years later, possibly during the rewrite when he "shortened" it. Such a trajectory is plausible, as he often rewrote and cannibalized his own material, and produced short story versions of at least three of his unpublished novels. Although it is difficult to see how it might derive from the same source, his short story "Dead Voices Live" might also then be a portion of this lost original, as that title is scrawled before "Tor. Vir" on the list. Although it incorporates characters and motifs that Keefauver employed several times in his work, including the unpublished novel *Shell*, "Dead Voices Live" itself did not see print until 1992, three years after Keefauver wrote his list (though the handwritten annotation may have been added later).